# Soul of a Monster

**Lock Down Publications and Ca$h Presents**

# Soul of a Monster

**A Novel by Aryanna**

**Lock Down Publications**
P.O. Box 870494
Mesquite, Tx 75187

**Visit our website**
**www.lockdownpublications.com**


First Edition June 2019
Printed in the United States of America



**Lock Down Publications**
**Like our page on Facebook: Lock Down Publications @**
**www.facebook.com/lockdownpublications.ldp**
Cover design and layout by: **Dynasty Cover Me**
Book interior design by: **Shawn Walker**
Edited by**: Kiera Northington**

# Stay Connected with Us!

Text **LOCKDOWN** to 22828 to stay up-to-date with new releases, sneak peeks, contests and more…

# Submission Guideline.

Submit the first three chapters of your completed manuscript to ldpsubmissions@gmail.com, subject line: Your book's title. The manuscript must be in a .doc file and sent as an attachment. The document should be in Times New Roman, double-spaced and in size 12 font. Also, provide your synopsis and full contact information. If sending multiple submissions, they must each be in a separate email.

Have a story but no way to send it electronically? You can still submit to LDP/Ca$h Presents. Send in the first three chapters, written or typed, of your completed manuscript to:

LDP: Submissions Dept
Po Box 870494
Mesquite, Tx 75187

*DO NOT send original manuscript. Must be a duplicate.*

Provide your synopsis and a cover letter containing your full contact information.

Thanks for considering LDP and Ca$h Presents.

# Dedication:

This book is dedicated to my soulmate because you love me even though you know what I am.

# Acknowledgements:

Father God, I thank you again for the opportunities you've given me, and for the talent you've blessed me with. I have to thank the love of my life for being my inspiration, my best friend, and my priest when I need to confess. I love you bae! I have to thank my kids for the love you give me, and for changing my life. There are no words to express what you mean to me, but know that I love you. I have to thank my family, especially my sister Big Byrd. I don't know when you became so wise, but I cherish every conversation we have. I can't wait to see you! I have to thank my fans and supporters for the continued love. I'm still here because of you, and that's not something I'll ever forget. I hope this story shows you that I'm still hungry to give you that street lit that'll keep you up at night. Helene I know you don't like it when I go crazy with the violence, but I promise the story is epic, so push thru for me. LOL! I have to thank my LDP fam for all the love and support as always. Cash I'ma show you how we make lightening strike twice in the same place, only this time we're gonna bottle that shit and sell it! Shout out to everybody behind the G-wall. I'ma keep telling stories for you, that's my word! Of course I gotta thank all of my haters for their dedication. I wish you health and long life because I need you! LOL! To anybody I forgot, you know not to take it personal…but you can if you want to. Free Dollar!!!

# Chapter 1
## Georgia
## August 2020

"Judge Kravens, Mrs. Kravens, it's so nice of you to have me over for dinner this evening, and the food is absolutely to die for. How did you get this pork shoulder so tender?" I asked, putting more of the delicious meat in my mouth.

"I-I just marinated it after I t-tenderized it," she replied.

"You're too modest, truly. I believe you can simply do magic in the kitchen," I said.

The couple didn't respond, but instead continued to watch me eat. I hadn't been lying to either of them when I was singing praises about her cooking, but it was obvious they wanted to have a different conversation.

"Maybe it's time that I explain why I've joined you tonight," I said, putting down my fork and knife and picking up my silenced Ruger 9mm pistol.

"Well, Judge, the story is long and boring, but I'll sum it up for you by saying you have information about a case I've been asked to look into."

"Wh-what case?" he asked cautiously.

"That would be the State of Georgia versus Delano Scotts on the count of—"

"I'm not presiding over that case," he interjected quickly.

"I never said you were the judge presiding over the case. I just said you have information about it. By that, I mean you can access the information I need because you work in the same building as the presiding judge, Theodore Ryan," I replied.

"What information do you need?" he asked.

"I need to know where the jurors are being sequestered to deliberate. As my luck would have it, none of their families knew their whereabouts."

"Jacob, you can't tell him that. If you do, he'll—"

Mrs. Kravens' opinion was suddenly silenced by a barely heard cough as a bullet pushed her face left and her thoughts to the right.

"Judge Kravens, you are now a widower, and I hate that for you. You've got a decision to make though and I'll be honest by telling you it's not an easy one. Either you can outlive your kids, or they can outlive you," I said simply.

I could see the wheels spinning in his head behind his eyes, no doubt wondering if I truly knew where little eight-year-old Jacob Jr. and seven-year-old Rachel really were, while their parents enjoyed date night. One look at his wife's remains told him it was best to assume that I knew all there was to know.

"I-I-I need my laptop, it's in-in the other room," he replied nervously, pointing towards his study.

"You've got twelve seconds to retrieve it and be back in that chair, or Melanie the babysitter will be my next stop," I warned, picking up my fork and continuing my meal.

I had to admit for his age, he shot out of that chair rather quickly. I knew exactly where his laptop was, so I knew it would take no more than eight seconds to retrieve it and return, but the extra four seconds was because I knew he'd grab the .38 he kept in a drawer.

"I'm glad that you didn't disappoint me," I said, continuing to eat as he appeared in my peripheral vision, with the gun outstretched in his trembling hand.

"Get-the fuck out of my house," he said forcefully.

"Jacob, I don't have time to waste, so sit down and let's get this over with."

"It's already over, motherfucka," he stated dramatically, pulling the trigger.

I simply stared at him with an expression of amused boredom riding my face.

"You know, for a white dude who is college educated and a law school graduate, you're not the sharpest knife in the drawer," I said.

Predictably, he pulled the trigger again and again, mystified that nothing was happening. While picking up another King's Hawaiian roll, I simultaneously took aim at his right kneecap, and made it disintegrate with two taps of the trigger. Naturally, he attacked the floor like they had a long history of domestic violence.

"Shut up all that damn racket, pick yourself and your laptop up, and get to work. This is the last time I'm gonna tell you," I said calmly.

It took him awhile to maneuver his girth up off the floor and into a chair, but I used the time to add more rice pudding and pork to my plate.

"Your wife really can cook, or at least she could," I said.

He was too busy crying to pay attention to me, but at least he was making progress on my request. I'd known it might take some convincing, because from all the research and spying I'd done on him, the judge was one of the few that wasn't corruptible. By all accounts, he was a good man, but that also made him a predictable man. In truth, that was part of the reason I'd taken out the firing pin to his pistol during one of my many excursions into his home. Also, I knew the look on his face would be comical. That look had paled in comparison to the shock that had blanketed his and his wife's face when a well-dressed, six foot three, two-hundred-and-forty-pound black man had taken a seat at their dinner table unexpectedly, hat in one hand, gun in the other.

It had been some “straight out of the movies” shit, or maybe straight out of their worst nightmares.

“Th-there,” he said, pushing the laptop towards me.

A quick look at the screen revealed the location of the hotel and the room numbers for each juror.

“Thank you,” I said, raising my pistol one more time and shooting him through his right eye.

After pulling out my phone to take a picture of the computer screen, I finished my meal in leisure. Not wanting to be an impolite guest, I loaded my dishes into the dishwasher and turned it on, before shutting down the judge’s laptop and returning it to his study. Satisfied with myself, I let myself out the back door and walked the three blocks to my 2020 forest green Navigator. Once I was secured inside, I peeled off my black latex gloves and put on a leather pair. With that done, I headed to my next location. It took me an hour to make the drive to the Holiday Inn Hotel in Buckhead, and upon arrival I sat in my truck, trying to figure out my strategy. Going in guns blazing was always fun, but probably not the most effective option I had to choose from. The security detail was probably light, considering that only the people in the positions of power knew where the jurors were hidden. But still, everybody didn’t need to die tonight. This thought went against everything I believed as a person, but this situation wasn’t about my personal beliefs. It was business, and the sole objective of this business was to get either a hung jury or an acquittal. For that, I only needed one person out of the eligible twelve in front of me, so I pulled my phone out to see whom fate would decide that lucky person was. I’d more or less memorized the detailed dossiers on each juror, but my review now was strictly to find the photo that spoke to me in this moment.

"Hmmm. You're kind of cute, Ms. Stacy Lattimore," I said aloud, admiring the smile that went all the way up to the blue eyes of the slender brunette. Once I had her room number, I put my phone back in my pocket and grabbed my briefcase off the backseat, before stepping out of my truck. My stroll inside the hotel was as casual as any other patron's, but my eyes scanned everything around me with the experience of a combat veteran. I'd never be arrogant enough to think that just because I killed without remorse or hesitation, that I was somehow bulletproof. I knew with certainty that death would come for me one day, and it wouldn't come with a peaceful smile or a gently touch. It would be ugly.

"Welcome to Holiday Inn, do you have a reservation?" a young black girl asked, once I'd reached the check-in desk.

"No, I don't. I'm actually just passing through on business, and I was hoping to get a room for the night," I replied, flashing her a disarming smile.

"No problem, sir, do you have an ID and a major credit card?

I quickly pulled out my wallet and provided her with what she needed.

"If possible, could you give me a room on the first floor?" I requested.

"Let's see…yes, sir. That can be arranged for you. It'll be sixty-four dollars and ninety-nine cents for the night. That comes with a complimentary breakfast, and check-out time is eleven am."

After I scribbled the signature that matched the fake ID and credit card, she passed me my documents back.

"Have a nice evening, Mr. Lawrence," she said with a smile.

I followed the arrows leading to room 116, after mistakenly going down the hallway where room 109 was. Surprisingly, there was no security in the hallway, but I wasn't about to complain. Once I was secured behind my door, I put my briefcase on the bed and popped it open. I quickly exchanged my silenced Ruger 9mm for a Taurus .380 with a silencer, closed the briefcase and slid it under the bed. A stop at the bathroom revealed that my dark blue Tom Ford suit still looked as fresh as it had when I'd put it on this morning, but the fedora I had on seemed out of place in this environment. To the casual observer, I had to be a businessman, not a pimp. Satisfied with my appearance, I tucked my gun and slipped quietly from my room. Within moments I was outside of room 109, tapping gently on the door.

"Who-who is it?" came a tentative voice.

"Simon and Patricia sent me," I replied, smiling.

I knew the use of her husband's and daughter's names would disarm her, because human nature trusted familiarity. Sure enough, within seconds, the door was being pulled open and I was greeted with a beautiful smile.

"Simon sent you?" she asked excitedly.

"I'm here on both your daughter and husband's behalf, I swear."

"Come in, come in," she said, ushering me into the room.

I stepped inside, quickly looking around to make sure the we were all by ourselves.

"I miss my family sooo much! I just want to see them and hold them close," she said dreamily.

"I have pictures for you," I replied, pulling my phone out, while taking a seat on the bed and beckoning her to me.

Once I had her particular file pulled up, I turned my phone over to her and let her scan through the random pictures of her family, out and about. I could tell she was so happy to see the people she loved and have some contact with the outside world, that it didn't register to her that these were surveillance photos. By the time she got to the last picture, I could tell she knew something was wrong.

"You-you said my family sent you with these pictures, but…they were taken like they weren't aware," she said slowly.

"I believe when I clarified myself, I stated I was here on their behalf and I promise you that I am, Stacy. Their lives are in your hands. Now, I could've come in here and stuck my gun in your face, beat up on you, raped you or worse, because all of those things are tools in my arsenal. I'm a person who very much believes that the ends justify the means, so I'll do whatever I feel is necessary to accomplish my goal. When I looked at your picture, I saw a reasonable woman who wouldn't let her civic duty come before what she loves most, so I decided to come to you with a reminder."

"I-I don't understand. What do you want?" she asked shakily.

"I want you to be able to go home to your husband and little girl. I want you to spend another Thanksgiving or Christmas with your mom and dad up in Colorado. I want you to continue to be that supportive voice for your sister, Elizabeth, when she comes to you with her marital problems. I truly want all of those things, but in order for all of that to remain reality, you have to do one thing. You gotta vote not guilty."

"Th-that's it? If I vote not guilty, you'll leave me and-and my family alone?" she asked, wiping the tears from her eyes.

"It will be as if I was a figment of your imagination," I assured her.

"Okay-okay, I can do that, just please don't hurt me or my family."

"Stacy, are you absolutely sure that you can vote not guilty and stick to it *no matter what* anyone else says to change your opinion."

"I'm p-positive, I swear I won't change my mind," she said quickly.

I stared deep into her pale blue eyes for a long time, not really looking for anything in particular, except to see how she handled my scrutiny.

"I want you to listen to me Stacy, I mean *really* listen to me because I'm gonna tell you the uncensored truth. I'm not the gangsta you see on TV, I'm not the dope boy you may ride past in Bankhead. I'm that thing that goes bump in the night. If you don't keep your word, you'll know exactly what that means," I promised.

She was crying too hard to talk, but she nodded her head emphatically to demonstrate her understanding.

"Good talk," I said, kissing her on the cheek and standing up.

I looked back at her when I got to the front door and I could tell she was shaken, but she looked like she'd be able to pull herself together. I let myself out of her room and ten minutes later, I was back behind the wheel of my truck pulling away from the hotel. Before I got too far away, I used my phone to make a call.

"It's done," I said, when the phone was answered.

"Okay. You up for something easy?"

"Send me the info."

# Chapter 2
## Two weeks later
## Florida

It never failed to amaze me how the Miami sunshine could make people throw their inhibitions to the wind and come out revealing a body that was not swimsuit ready. The sad part was that it wasn't just men either. There were actually women walking the streets built like bad cartoons and do TV ads that stressed the importance of quitting smoking. I hid my judgement behind my Ray-Ban's while navigating my candy purple, drop-top Chevy sitting on thirty-inch rims through the streets of Liberty City, but in my mind, I was talking plenty of shit. One good thing about travelling so much was that I got to see different people, places, and things, and that served to enhance my capabilities as a chameleon. I considered myself to be from nowhere and everywhere all at once, because I had the ability to be anyone, anywhere, at any time. My real name was something no one alive could speak, but the people who actually know me called me Dollar because that's what my late mother had called me. She'd given me that name because she said I had to much damn sense, but now it stood for the only master I would ever serve. I was 'bout that almighty dollar. It never mattered where I had to go or what I had to do in search of the bag, I secured it with ruthless efficiency, and I stacked my earnings like Scrooge McDuck. Not because I had a bunch of kids or family to leave my shit to when the end came, but because I'd missed too many meals to ever know hunger again. I pulled out my phone to verify the address I'd just cruised to a stop in front of and seeing it was the right spot made me shut the car off and hop out. I knew that no one would be able to spot the Glock .45 on my waist, and even though it gave me a familiar comfort, I still grabbed my duffle bag off my backseat. With my tan Dickies on, white t-shirt and black Chuck Taylors, I looked like any other nigga doing dirt in the hood, but I was really the last nigga you wanted to see. My stroll to the front door of the trap house was confident, just like my knock on the door.

"Who is it?" someone barked from the other side.

"Pablo sent me," I replied.

It took damn near a full thirty seconds to turn all the locks on the door, but finally it was opened, and I came face-to-face with a skinny white boy with dreadlocks.

"What's in the bag?" he asked.

"Your head if you don't move out the way," I said, walking past him into the dimly lit house.

I took my glasses off to let my eyes roam about while simultaneously taking in the layout. The stairs leading to the second floor were directly in front of me, and the living room was to my right. As I moved in that direction, I saw the kitchen down the hall, where two naked black chicks were cutting up a kilo of coke that was in front of them. The living room was only occupied by two other people, another slim white dude with dreads, and a white girl with dark brown hair.

"Which one of you is Chris?" I asked, dropping the duffle bag at my feet.

"That's me," the white boy on the couch said, raising his hand without taking his eyes off the sixty-inch TV screen taking up a wall.

"I'm Ronnie, and her name is Tabitha."

For the moment I ignored Tabitha, who was sitting on the couch, quietly smoking a blunt, and focused on Ronnie.

"Ronnie, is it?" I asked.

"Yeah I—"

His words suddenly got trapped when I grabbed him by his throat and pulled him towards me, while pulling the gun from my waist and sticking it in his open mouth.

"Shhhh, no talking. Ronnie, just listen," I whispered.

Despite Chris still being completely absorbed in his PlayStation, I could tell I had the man's undivided attention that was in front of me. I didn't really need him though, so I pulled the trigger and let his body drop before his brain matter could start working down the wall. My gun going off seemed to get everybody's attention.

"You ladies in the kitchen can keep working, this doesn't concern you. And Tabitha, you can keep smoking your blunt," I said.

"I had no intentions on stopping," she replied, smirking as she took another hit.

Her quick response actually humored me, but for the moment, someone else needed my attention.

"Chris, Chris, Chris, do you know why I'm here?" I asked.

"T-to collect Pablo's money and I got it, all of it, so you don't have to shoot me," he replied, clearly on the verge of terror.

"Pablo doesn't send a nigga like me to collect money for him, he only sends me to collect souls."

"That's gangsta," Tabitha said, around a mouth full of smoke.

"You have no idea," I said, smiling at her briefly.

"M-my soul? Why the fuck would Pablo wanna kill me?" Chris asked, in a voice several octaves above normal.

"It seems that you got into some legal trouble, and now you're offering up testimony on your co-defendant. Pablo can't be in business with a rat, so I'm the snake he sent to eat you," I replied.

"So gangsta," Tabitha said, chuckling now.

"What are you laughing about, bitch, he's gonna kill you too! You're a co-defendant on this case too!" Chris stated aggressively.

"She may be, but the only thing she ever told the people was *she didn't know shit*. You, on the other hand, gave details about the double homicide your friend committed, and that's where you fucked up," I said.

Tabitha's chuckles had turned into outright laughter now, which had a look of fury heating up Chris' face.

"He looks like he wants to hit you. Does he put his hands on you, Tabitha?" I asked.

Immediately, her laughter stopped and I could see painful memories cast a shadow over her face.

"Look, fuck that bitch. I've got all this money right here, and it's yours, just don't kill me," Chris pleaded.

When he leaned down to pick something up, I levelled my gun at him, but he moved slow like he had good intentions. Imagine my surprise when he came up holding something other than money, gold, or precious stones.

"Tabitha, is that your baby he's now holding in front of him like a shield?" I asked.

"Nope," she replied.

"Are either one of you ladies in the kitchen the mother to this baby?" I asked, looking at them.

Both women quickly shook their head no.

"He's my son and I'm all he's got. For his sake, let me live," Chris pleaded.

"Fool, you ain't got no kids with your little dick ass, stop lying," Tabitha said.

"Did you really just try to play on my humanity by bringing an innocent child into the equation?" I asked calmly.

The smile he gave me told me that in his mind, he still believed his play was gonna work.

"Tabitha, come unzip this bag and hand me what's inside," I demanded.

She was a little unsteady on her feet, but she managed to do what I asked so I didn't have to take my focus off the muthafucka in front of me.

"Thank you," I said, taking the double-barreled, sawed off 12-gauge from her hands.

I made sure to point this gun at Chris too while I tucked the other one back under my t-shirt.

"So, despite me having rearranged your man's thoughts just to change the wallpaper in this muthafucka, you think that baby in your arms will save you?" I asked seriously.

"You may be a killer, but shooting a baby is something totally different," Chris replied, standing more than a little confident.

"If you're right, and you're sure of that, then hold that beautiful baby boy up in front of you where I can't get a clean shot off," I said.

As soon as he did it, I cocked the hammers on the gun.

"You see, your problem is you see that baby as innocent and free of all the evils in this world, but you're forgetting the afterlife is filled with innocent souls. That baby's destiny was determined before he was born. Tabitha, if you have a weak stomach, I suggest you look away," I said seriously.

When her eyes locked with mine, I pulled the trigger and chopped father and son in half. I knew it was natural for her to jump, but what intrigued me was the lack of fear or disgust in her honey-colored eyes.

"Your eyes are beautiful," I said softly.

"Thank you."

"I'm not gonna kill you, nor will I insult you by telling you not to repeat what happened here today. Do you think I can give those chicks in the kitchen the same benefit, or do I need to kill them?" I asked.

"They were never here so they can be bought. I'll take care of it if you want," she offered.

"And why would you help me?"

"I'm helping myself. And maybe because you helped me. Sometimes it takes more than strong will to break an abusive cycle," she replied softly.

The pain that had been riding her face earlier was now floating through her eyes, explaining her statement without any more words.

"Thank you," I said.

"You're a gentleman."

"I was born a gangsta and a gentleman," I stated.

"Ah, so that's what you are. It definitely makes sense."

"No, that's who I was. What I am now is beyond words or definition," I said honestly, putting the shotgun back in my bag, and preparing to leave.

"Wait! You know there's money, dope, and guns in this house, right? You don't want it?" she asked curiously.

"Nah, I'm good."

"There's also cameras," she stated.

Hearing this caused my hand to hover over the doorknob as I turned to look back at her. I'd been given the details about the house and its occupants, but at no time was there any mention of cameras of any kind.

"Show me," I demanded.

Without hesitation, she led me into a dark bedroom directly across from the living room, where there was a desk holding up three different monitors full of images from various angles. I could see the bitches in the kitchen working, the bodies in the living room, and the gold flecks in my car's paint job.

"Is there a backup to this hard drive?" I asked.

"Not that I've ever seen, and I've been around awhile."

There was no doubt in my mind this set up was for security purposes but given Chris' inclination to be best friends with law enforcement, I also had little doubt that the proper authorities saw this footage. The only good news was that if it had been a live feed, I would at this very moment be engaged in a hell of a shootout. I quickly took a seat in front of the monitors, once again thankful for the time I'd spent learning at the feet of some legendary hackers. I got to work, erasing my entire existence from this moment in time.

"Do you mind if I take care of some stuff while you do that?" Tabitha asked.

"Are you gonna shoot me in the back while my attention is diverted?"

"No," she replied calmly.

"Then do what you gotta do."

Naturally, I watched her movements throughout the house for a solid three minutes before I was satisfied enough to shut the whole system down. Despite having erased everything, I still disconnected the hard drive and threw it in my bag with the wireless modem.

"I need a favor. I need a ride," Tabitha said, meeting me outside the bedroom door.

"You sure you wanna ride with me?"

"Are you gonna beat my ass or rape me?" she asked.

"No."

"Then we're good, as long as you don't mind a little baggage," she replied.

When I stuck my head out the door, I saw three duffle bags filled to bursting sitting on the floor against the wall. I dug my keys out of my pocket and handed them to her.

"That purple one is mine," I said.

Once she dragged the first two bags out, I pulled out my pistol and walked into the kitchen. I swiftly shot both women in the head, tucked my gun, picked up Tabitha's last duffle bag, and walked out without a backwards glance. By the time I got to my car, she was already sitting in the passenger seat, fucking with the radio. I tossed both bags in the backseat, hopped in the driver's seat, and pulled off. Mentally, I was supposed to be analyzing how I wanted to deal with the surprise in the form of surveillance that I'd walked into, but my mind kept drifting to my passenger. The only thing I knew about her was that she was different.

"Explain why you handle yourself so well under pressure," I said.

"Because I was raised in these streets, so all I know is pressure."

"Ain't no average white girl surviving the streets of Liberty City," I stated.

"First of all, I'm half Sicilian and Italian, but more importantly I ain't never been average. Not even my pussy is average."

Despite the seriousness on her face, I laughed because it was obvious that she believed in speaking her mind.

"You're a wild card, I can tell," I said.

"Oh, you have no idea."

"Aight, so where am I dropping you off?" I asked.

"Any hotel is good. I'll make arrangements from there."

"I got a better idea. I'll take you anywhere you wanna go, if you'll take a ride with me first," I bargained.

"Is that your way of asking for some pussy? I mean, I know we just went through some very intimate moments back there, but I don't even know your name," she replied, turning sideways in the seat so she was facing me.

"Intimate moments, huh? I like the way you put that, because killing is definitely an intimate thing but nah, I ain't asking for no pussy. Not even above-average pussy. I need to make a move real quick and I think it would go smoother with your help. I'm improvising."

"Something tells me this involves more killing," she said.

The look I gave her told her everything she needed to know.

"What's your name?" she asked.

"Dollar."

"I'm not talking about what the streets call you, I'm talking about the name your momma gave you," she said.

"That is the name my mom gave me, and the streets don't call me anything because to them, I don't exist. I like it that way."

"Okay. Well, Mr. Dollar, I'll take a ride with you on one condition," she replied.

"Oh yeah, what's that?"

"If I do you this favor, then you're gonna owe me one," she stated.

I knew I could've brought up the fact that I'd just spared her life, or that I'd given her free grabs over the spoils of war, but truthfully, I liked how she came at me. She had confidence, but it didn't come off as an arrogance to make deep seated insecurities.

"I'm good with that," I replied.

"Then I'm riding with you."

With that sealed, I pulled out my phone and sent a text to set my new plan in motion. A half an hour later I brought the car to a stop and turned in the seat to face her.

"Aight, we're getting ready to walk down the dock and step onto that nice sized yacht at the end. The man on board is a friend, but I still can't show up with a gun on me. I'm assuming you're wearing panties under that jean skirt, so I need you to tuck my .380 and silencer for me, and get them out when I give the signal," I said.

"It doesn't sound like we're going to visit a friend, but its whatever."

"Friends become enemies at a moment's notice," I replied, opening the glove compartment and passing her what she needed.

I averted my eyes while she handled the business of concealment and kept a close watch on our surroundings.

"So, what's the signal?" she asked.

"I'll tell you I love you."

"Nah, I don't want to hear that until you mean it. Pick something different," she insisted.

Again, she made me chuckle, but I liked her spunk.

"Aight, when you hear me say it's *all good,* then it's time for you to excuse yourself to the restroom. He keeps a personal bodyguard team of two, which means one might escort you, but just put the gun in his face and bring him to me. I'll handle the rest."

"I got you."

"Let's go," I said, putting my gun under the seat and stepping out of the car.

She followed my lead and I was able to look her over thoroughly to see if the gun was visible. I told myself that my admiring of her curves was all about how they helped her get away with hiding my pistol, but in truth, she was beautiful from head to toe. Her dark brown hair was naturally curly and had caramel highlights. She was short, maybe five foot four, and a hundred and fifty pounds, but it was put together in a way that made it clear nakedness would look wonderful on her.

"You know I can feel you checking me out, right?" she asked.

"I'm just making sure the gun ain't noticeable."

"Whatever you say. I look better with no clothes on though," she said, flashing me a devilish smile and taking my hand in hers.

I kept my mouth firmly shut so I wouldn't ask her if she'd read my mind. A few minutes later, we arrived at the yacht.

"I'm here to see Pablo," I stated to the dude built like an ex-body builder, in the ugly Hawaiian shirt.

"Hands up," he demanded.

I did like I was told so he could turn me around and frisk me, but I stepped in front of him when he moved towards Tabitha.

"That's my woman," I said.

"It's okay, baby, he can pat me down and show me to the bathroom while you handle business," she said, stepping around me and putting her arms up.

Under my careful observation, he barely touched her before pointing me in one direction while they went another. I found Pablo and his other bodyguard in the parlor watching a soccer game.

"My man, Dollar," Pablo said, standing to greet me.

"What's up, Pablo?"

"It's all good now, my friend," he replied.

"Yeah, we need to talk though because—"

My sentence was interrupted by the bodyguard's head suddenly exploding.

# Chapter 3

"I didn't mean to interrupt you, continue your conversation," Tabitha said, passing me the gun and sitting down to watch the soccer game.

"Don't touch anything, you're not wearing gloves," I said, pulling an extra pair from my pocket and tossing them to her.

"You're so thoughtful," she replied, smiling.

"Dollar, what the hell, man? What's going on?" Pablo asked, panicked.

On the streets, Pablo had the legend of some ruthless vato, but he was really a half Puerto Rican, half-white, trust fund baby who'd inherited his daddy's Columbian connections. Money could buy you hittas all day, which meant he could earn a reputation as a killa from the comforts of his yacht or his private jet. We both knew I was the truth when it came to killing though.

"Why didn't you tell me about there being cameras all over the house, Pablo? Think about your answer before you speak."

"C-cameras? I fucking forgot about the cameras!" he replied, slapping his forehead dramatically.

"You forgot? That's the story you're gonna go with?" I asked.

"That's a weak story, Pablo," Tabitha said, picking up a club sandwich from the spread on the table in front of her.

"It's the truth! Come on, Dollar, you know me, and we've been doing business for years," he insisted.

"Probably not a good time to bring up that you know where the bodies are buried, Pablo. That makes you a liability," she said, around a mouthful of food.

"Bitch, *shut up*! Dollar knows I would never betray him!"

His decision to call Tabitha out of her name got both of his kneecaps blown off.

"I'm just wondering if you're working with the cops too, or if I was gonna be your fall guy," I said, over his high-pitched begging.

"Dollar, I would never, I would nev—"

Three bullets to the face stopped him from talking.

"Come on, let's go," I said, tucking the gun in my waist.

"These sandwiches are amazing," she said, grabbing another one and following me. I dropped my phone in the water once we'd made it a couple boats down, thereby severing any ties to the late Pablo, except for the gun I would later dismantle.

"So, where to?" I asked, once we were back in the car.

"Alabama, Tuscaloosa to be exact."

I looked over at her to see if she was bullshitting, but she was serious.

"Okay. My next question is, where are we stashing all the shit you got in the back while we make this road trip?"

"That kind of depends on whether you were gonna drop me off or not," she replied.

"You know I'm pretty sure you've got the money in one of those bags to rent and or buy a car. Then, you don't have to worry about a ride."

"You're right, but it's more important to me to know that you're a man of your word on *all things*, and you did say that you'd take me where I wanna go. Plus, given everything that's happened today it's probably a good idea to put Florida behind me, and for there to be no trace of how I felt," she said.

It was hard to argue with her logic, but the strange part was that I really didn't want to. I didn't relish the thought of riding filthy from state to state, but I was a man of my word.

"Aight then," I said, starting the car and putting the top up before pulling off.

"Don't you need to go to your spot and get your stuff?" she asked, once she saw that I was hopping straight on the highway.

"Nah, I travel light like a salesman."

"A salesman, huh? Somehow, I don't envision you peddling Avon products, insurance, or vacuum cleaners," she said, laughing.

"Not hardly."

"Do you smoke weed?" she asked, finishing up the last of her sandwich, and pulling her gloves off.

"Occasionally."

My response was enough to have her climbing into my backseat, where she stayed for ten minutes. The smell of good ganja preceded her return to riding shotgun.

"So, where do you live?" she asked, passing me the blunt.

"Everywhere."

"Given your obvious profession, I know you're not homeless, so should I take that to mean you've got a place in every state?" she asked.

"No, it just means I stay on the move too much to ever really put down roots."

"On the move or on the run?" she asked, seeking clarification.

"I don't run."

"Mmm, you definitely don't seem like the type to run or be shaky, Mr. Dollar."

"You either, Ms. Tabitha," I replied, passing the blunt back.

"You know you don't have to call me by my government name, right?"

"Okay, so what would you prefer I call you?" I asked.

"I'm sure you can think of something."

The sexiness in that statement increased the temperature in the car by at least ten degrees, but I maintained my cool.

"I like your eyes, so I think I'll call you Honey," I said, thoughtfully.

"Honey, huh? I guess it's a good thing that you didn't see my nipples first, or you'd be calling me Pinky."

My laugh was instantaneous and natural, and the weed only made it funnier.

"Do you always say what's on your mind?" I asked, accepting the blunt back.

"Yeah, ain't no need to hide it. Plus, I'm funny as fuck sometimes."

"I don't doubt that for a second, Ms. Honey."

As the miles and hours ticked by, I found out just how funny she was. It was foreign to me to laugh this much and kick it with someone I barely knew so easily, but it was happening. Given everything that had happened, and the close quarters we were sharing, getting to know each other happened at a scary speed. Of course, I didn't reveal much, but I listened to everything because she was interacting. There was serious conversation in between the jokes, and the shit she'd been through in life told me she embodied the definition of the word survivor. I didn't pity her though for her experiences. I felt her. It was about nine hours before we crossed over into Alabama, and I pulled over at the first motel that I came to.

"I'll help you carry all this stuff inside once we check-in, and then I'll go get us something to eat," I said.

"Or, you could just order a pizza."

"I'm not gonna abandon you, don't worry," I said half-jokingly.

"I didn't say you were. I just know that you've gotta be incredibly tired, so I think it's best we hold up for the night. Do you got something against pizza?"

"No, I don't have anything against pizza. Wait right here," I replied, getting out of the car and going inside the Best Western.

Within ten minutes, I had us a room with two beds in it, and I was unloading the car while she ordered our food. In truth, I was tired, but I was also anxious to get back to work. Taking lives wasn't just about the money for me. My dirty little secret was that I *liked* killing, because it spoke to something inside me on a primal level. I wasn't interested in the psychobabble that college professors would spew about why I did what I did. I was only interested in the joy it brought me. Only a crazy person would choose not to do something they loved, especially when they were getting paid for it.

"I didn't know what you liked on your pizza, so I got half-cheese, half-everything," Honey said, once I'd come back into the room and shut the door.

"Please tell me that when you say everything, you don't mean pineapples too."

"Where *you* been eating pizza?" she asked, laughing.

"Trust me, I've seen some weird shit all over the place."

"Apparently. Don't worry, there's no weird shit coming on our pizza, but I did get an extra-large because you look like you can eat," she said, smiling.

"You know I can feel you checking me out, right?"

"Yeah, well, I'm not gonna come up with some lame ass excuse like you did," she replied laughing.

I laughed with her, even though I knew I was admitting to checking her out.

"I'ma keep it one hundred, you're beautiful. After getting to know you though, I gotta say that you remind me of an old Kanye West album, *Beautiful Dark Twisted Fantasy*," I said.

"Well, you really know how to give a bitch a compliment! Nah, I'm just fucking with you. I like the way you put that, plus that was before Kanye lost his damn mind and forgot how to make good music."

"Don't even get me *started* on that nigga," I said, shaking my head in frustration.

"I won't, but I would like to get started on this inventory, and I'd like your help," she replied, grabbing a duffle bag and putting it on one of the beds.

I grabbed one and took it to the other bed. I unzipped it to find money, a staggering amount of money because I hadn't thought Chris was moving product like that but apparently, I was mistaken.

"Is it too late to ask for half?" I asked, jokingly.

"No, you can have half."

Her response had been immediate, but what kind of threw me off was that she was being sincere, and I could tell by the look in her eyes.

"I was only fucking with you," I said.

"Don't fuck with me, *fuck with me* because you'll never find a bitch that's realer."

Even with me only knowing her a short time I had little doubt about the truth she was speaking. Our eyes stayed fixed on each other for what seemed like an eternity, but a sudden knock at the door broke the trance and had her reaching for a chrome Berretta 9mm.

"If it's all the same to you, I'd rather pay for the pizza, it'll be less of a mess that way," I said, grabbing a few bills from out of the bag in front of me, and going to the door.

Once I was sure she wasn't gonna shoot, I opened the door and quickly paid for the pizza. I sat it on the bed next to her, took a slice, and went back to the job I'd been tasked to do.

"Okay, so I'm a little jumpy," she admitted, sheepishly.

"It's been a long day," I said, dumping the entire contents of the duffle bag on the bed.

I'd thought there was only money in this bag, but suddenly I was looking at her lace panties and bras. I might've been content to simply stare for a moment if something else hadn't caught my eye.

"Is this yours?" I asked, sitting my slice of pizza down, and picking up the carrying case that had come open.

Inside was a needle, a spoon, and a baggie of powder that I was gonna make an educated guess to be heroin. Without a word, she stepped over to me, took the case from my hands and went back to her bed. I fought the urge to say something by putting my pizza back in my mouth and distracting myself by separating Victoria's Secrets from the cash. Once I had that done, I went to grab another piece of pizza, but I pulled up short at the sight of the tears sliding soundlessly down her face. It was pure instinct that made me turn her towards me, take her face in my hands, and kiss the trail of her tears until they were no more.

"The demons you fight are yours, which means I'm not qualified to judge how you choose to fight them. You're stronger than that though," I said, nodding towards the heroin.

She nodded her head slightly, but I could still see the tears in her eyes. I'd never seen sadness come with such beauty because it was like looking at the sunset under water. I wanted to kiss her and maybe she was expecting me to, but instead, I let her go and took a step back.

"I'm gonna run out and grab a few things, do you need me to bring you anything back?" I asked.

"N-no, I'm good."

I grabbed a slice of pizza and headed out the door. The first thing that I did when I got in the car was break down the dirty .380 so I could toss it and put my .45 back on my hip. With that done, I pulled off in search of a place to buy a new burner phone so I could call my accountant. My decision to leave Honey alone wasn't because I was incapable of feeling or sympathizing, it was about giving her a choice on whether or not to be that vulnerable with me. Our lives had come crashing together unexpectedly, but it wasn't right for me to force her to reveal her ugliest truths to me. It only took me twenty minutes to get rid of the gun and get a new phone, but I sat in the car a little longer to give her some time. Plus, it was time to get back to work.

"It's me," I said, once my call was answered.

"What took you so long to check in? I was worried."

"Sorry, something unexpected happened," I replied.

"Yeah, I heard something about that. I hope you had a good reason, because you just upset the natural order for *a lot* of people."

"Couldn't be avoided," I said shortly.

"Whatever you say. Are you taking a vacation?"

"Have I ever?" I retorted.

"Okay, well, you're needed in Chicago."

"I'll be there," I replied, hanging up.

Part of me wanted to go into my encrypted email now and find out whom it was that needed killing, but I knew it could wait until after I dropped Honey off tomorrow. So, I got out of the car and headed back to the room. When I let myself in, I didn't see Honey anywhere, but I heard the shower running. The bed she'd been working on had seven kilos of cocaine, five pistols, and what looked to be about one hundred thousand dollars in cash all neatly organized. The bed I'd been stationed at had at least double the amount of cash, all stacked in different denominations. I ate another slice of pizza while admiring her efficiency, but I almost choked on it when the bathroom door opened and she stepped out of the fog.

"The water is still hot," she said, using the towel in her hand to dry her hair. My focus wasn't on her hair though. It was completely captivated by her gorgeous naked body. My eyes greedily took in every inch of her, from her light pink, quarter-sized nipples to her tiny manicured toes.

"Damn, you're sexy," I stated.

"Oh, there's more," she replied, turning around so that I could see just how juicy her ass really was.

The smile on her face told me that she knew the effect she was having on me, and she loved it.

"The water is still hot?" I asked, pulling my gloves off and my t-shirt over my head.

"Uh-huh."

I dropped what I'd been holding on the floor as I kicked my shoes off and put my gun on the table. The look in her eyes was no longer one of teasing flirtation, but building hunger. This made me unbuckle my belt slower and take my time pushing my pants and boxers to the floor. Her eyes locked in on my dick like it was a lighthouse in the fog guiding her in from the sea.

"Interesting," she said softly, licking her lips.

Once I took off my socks, I walked right up on her and stood in front of her long enough to smell the soap on her skin.

"Thanks," I said, taking the towel from her hand as I moved past her into the bathroom.

I didn't hear the door close until I was beneath the water's spray, but I wasn't disappointed that she didn't join me. The art of seduction was always intriguing. It took fifteen minutes before any trace of hot water vanished, forcing me out of the shower. When I stepped back into the room, I found another surprise because both beds had been cleared off.

"I didn't know which bed you were sleeping in…so I decided to push them together," she said, her voice laced with pure sexiness.

The fact that she made this statement while sitting on the side of the bed facing me, with her legs spread wide open, and her fingers exploring the inner secrets of her body, made my heart beat faster.

"Wh-what are you doing?" I asked.

"Waiting on you. I'm gonna show you how this honey turns to gold."

# Chapter 4

The way she slowly pushed her index and middle fingers as far as they would go inside her pussy had me transfixed in a way porn could never accomplish. The fact that I could hear the suction of her pussy just from a little finger popping had me nervous, because that sound signified just how tight she was. I thought her nipples had been a pretty pink, but the flower she was opening in front of me was vibrant in color and wetter than the Pacific. Without a doubt, I was gonna need that sweetness on my tongue.

"Don't move," she said, halting my forward progress.

"You want me to watch?"

"For now, yeah. My pussy is pretty, huh?" she asked seductively.

"You know it is."

"You're right, I do know. I know it's good too," she said, pulling her fingers out long enough to suck her juices off, and then going back to work.

Her eyes went down to my dick, but I could already feel what she could see. That mufucka was pointing at her like a referee signaling first down.

"See something you like?" I asked.

"You know I do."

"You're right, I do know. How long are you gonna make me wait to give it to you?" I asked, making it jump without lifting a finger.

"N-not long," she whispered, moving her hand faster now.

Ignoring her earlier command, I took two steps towards her, which put me close enough to her that I could breathe the air she was exhaling. I didn't touch her though or make a move like I intended to, I just watched.

"Lay down and spread your legs wide," I instructed.

As soon as she laid back, I noticed the trembling in her legs.

"Oh-shit! Shit! D-Dollar, I'm cumming!" she moaned loudly.

My mouth was too dry to say anything. All I could do was watch and wait.

"Ahhh-fuck!" she yelled, rubbing her clit rapidly.

What happened next, I couldn't have prepared for if she'd given me any type of warning, but the fact that she *didn't* warn me only made it sexier. Her pussy didn't simply gush from her climax, it squirted and some of it landed on my thigh. For a second, I just looked down in amazement, and then I ran my finger through her cum on my leg before bringing it to my mouth and tasting it.

"You were right, it is good," I said huskily, closing the distance between us.

My dick hurt from my desire to be inside her, but the taste of her deliciousness on my tongue had my head in between her legs. I started by kissing and licking all traces of her cum off of her inner thighs, and then I focused my attention on the main course.

"Mmm, eat this pussy, baby," she purred, propping her legs up on my shoulders.

I could still feel the throbbing of her clit when my lips locked on it, and the moment I started sucking, her back bent like a boomerang. Just when she thought she could handle the sucking I switched up and let my tongue give her the run around.

"Dollar!" she moaned passionately.

"Shhh," I breathed, right up against the pussy so she could feel the vibrations.

When I stuck my finger inside her wet, tight, warm pussy I felt it throbbing like someone was playing a drum solo in dedication to her G-spot. My pace was slow enough to make time stand still, but I licked, sucked, and nibbled on her delicious pussy until a blinding light ripped her world in half. I didn't even let her catch her breath before flipping her over, and putting her on her hands and knees. The trembling that I'd noticed before her first climax was nothing compared to the way she was shaking now, but I had no mercy to give.

"You ready?" I asked, rubbing the head of my dick back and forth across her pussy lips.

"Fuck me!" she demanded savagely.

I gave her the first two inches nice and slow while wrapping her long hair around my hand, but once I had a firm grip, I dove inside with force and purpose. I heard the air rush from her lungs, and before she could breathe again, I hit her with another stroke of matched intensity.

"Goddamn," I mumbled, when she used all her strength to grip my dick.

I had no choice except to slow down, but I didn't want to. I wanted to run my dick through her until it came out of her mouth, but for now I enjoyed the pace of give and take.

"P-punish me," she said suddenly.

"What?"

"P-punish me, daddy, f-fuck me harder," she begged.

Without hesitation, I grabbed her hair tighter, forcing her to look at the ceiling while my other hand went to her hip and I held her steady. I pulled back until just the head of my dick was pulsating inside her and then I pounded her with long strokes that had her cheeks wobbling like ripples across a pond. With each blow, I could feel the sky inside her getting darker, matching my own as the storm of fulfillment came closer. As the clouds parted I moved faster, fucking her with force and speed that had my heart thundering inside my chest.

"D-Dollar, I'm—"

"Me too, Honey!" I growled, exploding inside her at the same instant she drenched me with her orgasm.

It hadn't been my intention to collapse, but when her knees gave out, I landed on top of her.

"My-my bad," I said, laughing.

"I can't-I can't feel anything right now," she replied, chuckling.

It took a lot of effort for me to roll out of her and onto my back, but I finally accomplished it.

"That was un-expected," I admitted.

"You ain't never lied. Did you really eat my pussy first though?"

"Why do you sound surprised?" I asked, looking at her.

"Because most muthafuckas want head, first, second *and* third, then they want pussy and ass, and *maybe* after that they'll lick the pussy in a half-assed sort of way."

"I ain't most muthafuckas, I thought that was obvious by now," I replied.

"Oh, it was before, but I'd swear to it under oath now. As soon as I catch my breath, I'ma show you the magic my mouth can do."

"Sure, you will, your ass is already yawning," I said, laughing softly.

"Fuck you, I ain't had no dick like that in…shit, I don't know that I have, but don't let that go to your head because I'm getting my run back," she replied, scooting closer to me until she could rest her head on my chest.

"Am I trippin' or are your eyes really gold?"

"I told you I was gonna show you how this Honey turns gold. Whenever I cum, my eyes change colors," she said.

"That's sexy, so is the way you squirt when you cum. *That shit* turned me on."

"If I had more time, I bet I could turn you out, have you feigning for this good pussy," she replied, chuckling.

"Or you'd end up sprung on this good dick," I countered.

"This shit is crazy though. If you would've told me when I woke up this morning that this was how my day would end, I would've asked what size straight jacket you wear. I don't give the pussy up to strangers, and I damn sure don't tell them all my business like I've done with you."

"Yeah, I feel you. I don't typically leave witnesses alive," I said seriously.

Her response to that comment wasn't immediate so I figured that she was probably replaying all the shit that happened since we'd met.

"Why do you kill people?" she asked suddenly.

"Because, people need killing. And, because I like it."

"Wow. I didn't expect you to be that honest," she replied.

"Why not? It's what I chose to do, so there's no reason to be ashamed of it."

"So earlier it didn't bother you at all when, when you, uh, when—"

"When I killed that baby," I finished for her.

"Yeah that. You weren't bothered?"

"Empathy, pity, and mercy are things I don't have the luxury of indulging in. I learned long ago that the only people who play by the rules in the streets are those pretending. They're halfway crooks. Think about how many muthafuckas play by rules or some code of honor, only to have it come back and bite them in the ass. I decided long ago the price to pay for that mistake was too high, and I made the decision to be ruthless about my self-preservation. I also made the decision to commit to what I do because second guessing would make me no different than those halfway crooks," I replied.

"So, then what makes me special? Because, based on what you said, my size six and a half should be wearing a toe tag," she asked, looking up at me.

For a moment, I just stared into her eyes, letting her question reach every corner of my mind before I said anything.

"The truth is, I don't know. I've never done it before though. I've never connected with a female the way that I have with you, and I can't explain that either. All I know is that I survive because of my instincts and my ability to read people, and I ain't got no bad vibes from you yet."

"Surprisingly, I ain't got none from you either, even though you do what you do. So, what do you think this means?" she asked.

"At this point I'm not overanalyzing it, or at least I wasn't before this conversation started," I replied, smiling.

"So, we're just gonna take life as it comes, huh?"

"They say that life is ten percent what happens to you and ninety percent how you react to it," I stated.

"What the hell do *they* know," she said, getting up off the bed.

I didn't know what she was doing, but I didn't mind watching her sexy ass move around. After she turned the bathroom light off, she grabbed my gun off the table, and turned the room lights off too. I could see her moving towards me in the slivers of moonlight leaking through the blinds, and I felt her weight back on the bed. Once she put my gun under one of the pillows, she resumed her position on my chest, snuggling up to me.

"I can't remember the last time I cuddled with a woman," I said.

"Me either, but good sex will make you do some weird shit."

We both laughed softly because denying it would've been pointless.

"Goodnight," she said, kissing my chest gently.

"Sweet dreams," I replied, wrapping my arms around her.

I thought it would take me awhile to get to sleep like it did almost every night, but no sooner had I heard her deep breathing I found myself drifting off into a peaceful rest. I don't know how long I stayed that way, but I knew instantly what woke me up. When I opened my eyes and looked down, her eyes were staring back at me, glowing like a wild cat in the jungle, but she didn't have prey in her mouth. She had me. What started out as a tease with her only sucking the head, and then licking slowly down my shaft before starting over, morphed into the sweetest torture. Before I knew it, my hands were wrapped up in her hair, I was moaning her name, and pumping cum down her throat like gasoline. When it was over, I couldn't speak and she simply cuddled back up to me. Within minutes, I was sleep again. The next time I opened my eyes, I found her still sleeping soundly, despite the daylight shining all around us. I feared that she was a light sleeper and would wake up when I tried to move, but I managed to slide from beneath her without the slightest change in her breathing. I'd never watched anyone sleep, but she was too beautiful to take my eyes off of. The problem was the longer I stood there, the more I thought it was stupid to waste good morning wood. I slowly turned her over on her back and carefully wrapped her legs around my waist while easing my dick inside her.

"Good morning, Honey," I whispered, when her eyes snapped open and locked on me.

"It-it is good."

My strokes were slow, yet thorough enough for the pleasure they caused to be evident by the beautiful expression on her face. I could tell by the look in her eyes she knew that this experience was different from last night, but she was okay with that. Without breaking stride, I brought my lips to her neck and kissed her tenderly, working my way up to her earlobe, where I bit her softly. After doing the same to her other ear, I pulled back until my face was hovering inches about hers. It was amazing to see her eyes begin their transformation, like the sun leaving footprints across the sky in the evening. I'd seen a lot of things in my life, but nothing like this.

"You're gorgeous," I whispered.

When she opened her mouth to reply, I brought our lips together for the first time and from that point on, we communicated without words. Even when we climbed, we did it with our lungs joined, breathing the same air, while our hearts beat out a message of unity. When it was over, I stayed on top of her, inside of her, trying to stare past the beauty of the gold looking back at me so I could catch a glimpse of her essence.

"Why did you kill the bodyguards when we were on the yacht?" I asked.

"Because it needed to be done and from a practical standpoint, it made the most sense that I do it."

"It didn't bother you?" I persisted.

"Based on what you told me, it was obvious that their death was necessary for us to make it off that boat alive. I'm a survivor, and that will never bother me."

I kissed her again before finally getting off of her.

"You wanna shower first while I go get breakfast?" I asked.

"No, I wanna shower together and we'll get breakfast once we're back on the road," she replied, standing up and grabbing ahold of my dick.

She then proceeded to lead me to the shower, and we didn't remerge for a long forty-five minutes. Of course, neither of us was complaining though. It only took us twenty minutes to get dressed, load up, and get back on the move. Part of me was looking forward to getting to Chicago, but there was an alien feeling overlapping my usual enthusiasm about killing. I couldn't put a name on the feeling, but I knew it existed because I was feeling my passenger. We talked for the two hours it took to get to her destination, but we both knew that there was a lot we weren't saying.

"You can pull over right there," she said, pointing to a spot at the curb.

I thought the house she wanted was the one on my side, but her head was turned towards a red brick one across the street from where we sat. I put the car in park and turned the engine off, waiting on her to make the next move. After a while, she turned sideways in the seat with her back facing me and slid towards me, until I wrapped my arm around her.

"Who lives there?" I asked, staring out the window with her.

"My parents and my two youngest kids."

"Rain and Ray-Ray," I said.

"You really were listening to me talk, huh? Yeah, this is where they stay."

"Won't they be surprised to come home from school to see you," I said.

"Right...they have a good life here though."

"And you have the means to give them a better life right in the backseat," I assured her.

"It takes more than money to give them a good life, especially when I don't have my shit all the way together," she replied.

I wanted to tell her that I thought she'd be an incredible mother and provider no matter what she was going through, but I sensed that this was a time for me to listen, whether she spoke in words or silence.

"You know that favor you owe me?" she asked, a few minutes later.

"Yeah."

"I think I'm gonna call it in now," she said, pulling her phone out of her pocket.

"Whatever you need."

She quickly dialed a number and waited for an answer.

"H-hi, Mom…yeah, it's really me. I'm fine, how is everyone there? I'll be coming to visit soon, I promise. I miss you all too. Mom, I'm making some major changes in my life, and once that's done I'll come home, okay? Yes, I promise to call more until then. The reason I'm calling now is because a friend of mine is bringing something to you for me, just something to show my appreciation for all that you and Dad have done. I love you both too…listen, I've gotta get back to work, but I'll call back soon, make sure you tell everyone I love them…bye, Mom."

I didn't need to ask her if she was okay because I could feel her tears falling like raindrops on my arm. I understood that words would give no comforts, so I held her tighter instead.

"I need you to take a duffle bag to the house over there," she said.

"I can do that."

Slowly she unwrapped from my embrace and climbed into the backseat. Ten minutes later, she handed me a bag with two hundred thousand dollars in it, and I was out of the car on my way to meet the parents. It struck me as funny how I'd never met the parents of a female I was fucking in all of my thirty-five years in this world, and here I was about to drop damn near a quarter of a million dollars on Honey's. I took a deep breath and rang the doorbell, and a few moments later I came face-to-face with a slightly older version of the woman ducked down in the car behind me.

"Hi, I'm a friend of Hon-I mean, Tabitha's. She asked me to bring this to you," I said, passing her the bag.

She stared at me warily, before taking the bag and opening it. When she looked back up at me, her face was so distraught that you would've sworn it was a severed head in the bag.

"Where is she? She's in trouble, isn't she? Please tell me where she is and if she's okay."

"She's still in Florida and she's not in any trouble, I promise. She's been working hard and saving all her money, and she wanted you to have some," I said reassuringly.

"You swear she's not in any kind of trouble?"

"I give you my word that she's not in any trouble, and she won't be," I replied.

She stared at me for a long moment without saying anything.

"What's your name, young man?"

"Dollar."

"Well, Dollar, I don't know you, but if my daughter trusted you to bring me this much money and you did it, then you're obviously a man of character. So now, I'm gonna ask you to do something for me."

"What's that?" I asked curiously.

"Protect my daughter. No man in her life has ever done that, but it's obvious she's putting faith in you, and so I'm gonna do the same. Will you protect my daughter, Dollar?"

"Yes, ma'am," I replied without hesitation.

Once she was satisfied that I was telling the truth, she gave me a brief hug before stepping back into the house and closing the door. It wasn't until I was walking back to the car that I asked myself what the hell I'd just done.

"I feel like I would've paid another two hundred thousand dollars to be a fly on the wall. What were you two talking about?" Honey asked, once I was back in the driver's seat.

"One day I might tell you, but for now, I'd like to know what your next move is."

"I don't know, what's yours?" she countered.

"Somebody needs killing in Chicago."

"Then we go to Chicago," she said.

# Chapter 5
## Two days later
## Chicago

"Father Brennan, we know it's short notice, but we're so in love, and we can't wait another moment to get married," Honey said excitedly, taking my hand as she looked across the desk at the preacher.

"Love is beautiful and glorious thing my children, but your request is highly unorthodox since you are not members of my church," Father Brennan replied.

"But we are devoted Catholics, and since we decided to get married just this very morning, it only made sense to choose a Catholic church. Father Brennan, God led us to you," Honey said sincerely.

It took everything in me to keep a straight face, but it was clear to me that Honey missed her calling, because she should've been on the big screen.

"What type of ceremony were you thinking about, Honey?" Father Brennan asked.

"Something intimate, just us and maybe a few witnesses. We don't have any family, except for our church back home, so we were hoping that you had some good Catholics around to witness another miracle union," Honey replied.

"Well, right now, I'm the only one here. But afternoon mass will be in about an hour and a half, so a few members of the church will be here," he said.

I gave Honey's hand a gentle squeeze because we had the information we needed.

"Father, we would very much appreciate you fitting us into your busy schedule, and we would like to make a small donation to the church for the invaluable time spent here," I said, pulling ten thousand dollars out of my suit jacket pocket, and placing it on his desk.

The greed in his eyes quickly turned the brown hue to an almost emerald green, but that didn't surprise me. It had been my experience that people in the positions of religious authority fall victim to the seduction of immediate gratification quicker than the average person on the street. They could give sermons all day on the book of Job and how suffering doesn't happen in vain when you have faith and patience. But in the dark, they answered to the weakness of the flesh too. Father Patrick Brennan was no different. In fact, he was worse.

"Well-uh-that is mighty generous of you both. Am I to assume you have a valid marriage license?" he asked, making the money disappear faster than any magic act I'd ever seen.

"I'll run out to the car to get it," I said, kissing the back of Honey's hand as I stood up.

I could hear her continuing the charade by discussing a ceremony in the garden as I closed the door and made my way outside to the parking lot. My pace wasn't hurried, but my eyes scanned everything like windshield wipers on high gear. Nothing appeared out of the ordinary, and that allowed me to grab my duffle bag from the trunk of my white 1998 Pontiac Bonneville, before retracing my steps back into the church. Even though Father Brennan acknowledged my return, I could tell that Honey had his undivided attention. Undoubtedly, it was probably because her all-white summer dress hugged her upper body like a second skin, and it looked like the odds of her titties popping out was a better than fifty-fifty chance. Honey's beauty was undeniable for any man or woman, and even though she had the body of a twenty-something at thirty-eight years old, I knew she was too old for him, much too old. I discreetly locked the door before moving to the old oak desk that Father Brennan was sitting behind and put my duffle bag right in front of him. I quickly reached inside, pulled out four zip ties and passed them to Honey.

"Hands and feet," I ordered.

"Wh-what's this?" Father Brennan asked.

In response, I took my snub nose .45 revolver out of the bag and put it right in between his eyes.

"This, Patrick, is what I refer to as God's plan. Being a man of the cloth, I know that you have enough faith to know God doesn't make mistakes, right?"

"R-r-right," he replied shakily.

"Good, so then let's just see how this plays out, because whatever is meant to be will be."

Once Honey had his limbs secured tightly, I sat the gun down and removed the rest of the necessary tools from my bag. With that done, I strapped a ball gag on Patrick and prepared to get to work.

"If you will forgive us for our earlier deception, Father, I'll explain how we really came to be here on this glorious morning. I'm here, Father, because you have sinned and this is your moment of atonement. Now, I won't lie to you, there won't be any reprieve in the form of Hail Mary's for you to receive absolution for these sins you have committed. You must pay with your life," I said gravely.

Immediately, he started trying to talk around the ball in his mouth, but I waved his mumblings off.

"I know, I know, you want to beg and plead, and reason with me to spare your life for one reason or another, but the truth is that all that is a waste of time. Would you like to know why?" I asked.

Following the shaking of his head in the affirmative, I looked over at Honey. She slowly and deliberately picked up the pair of garden shears off the desk, slid Father Brennan's left index finger in between the blades, and severed it from his hand in a merciless fashion.

"You should *never* have touched those kids, Patrick," she whispered sweetly.

"You're so beautiful," I said, admiring everything about her in this moment.

She smiled brightly at me, but I could see in her eyes that some of her demons had swam to the surface. She hadn't told me exactly what happened to her in her past, but from the moment I'd told her why Patrick Brennan had to die, she'd insisted on being a part of it. I'd never had a partner in the field before, because I put my life in no one's hands except my own, but being here with her in this moment felt so right that I wouldn't question it. Instead, I would enjoy it.

"Patrick, I can tell by the look in your eyes that you wanna plead your innocence and swear on a stack of Bibles that you never touched even one child inappropriately. The truth is that you've molested dozens though. You used your position as a giver of hope to change and destroy lives, and now you want me to listen to you plead for yours?" I asked.

He was mumbling and crying, but I was already nodding at Honey to add his next finger to the bloody one staining the carpet.

"Did you listen to the children's pleas, Father? Or did you look into their scared and confused eyes, and convince them that God approved of your behavior?" Honey asked, quickly clipping his ring finger also before I could give the go ahead.

I could tell by the dazed look in Patrick's eyes that he wasn't planning to be conscious for long, so I pulled the top off of the syringe I had and administered a healthy dose of adrenaline.

"Can't have you leave your own party. Now, where were we?" I asked.

"Right about *here,"* Honey replied, adding the pinky finger to the growing pile on the floor.

When I looked at her, I could see that whatever demons she'd been fighting had completely consumed her and if she wasn't careful, she'd drown.

"Honey, come here," I said, holding out my hand to her.

"Huh?" she asked, confused.

"I said, come here."

Reluctantly, she put the shears on the desk and stepped around the chair until she was standing in front of me.

"It's okay," I whispered, pulling her into my arms.

For a second she just looked up at me blindly, and then her tears fell with the weight and speed of a ship's anchor. Her eyes held so much pain that it caused a physical reaction in me, forcing me to wrap my arms around her tighter. We stayed like that until I felt her body stop trembling, and then I leaned down to touch my lips to hers.

"You're okay," I said softly.

"I know. I need you to do something for me."

"What is it, sweetheart?" I asked.

"Fuck me."

"Y-you mean right now?" I asked slowly.

"Yeah, right here, right now. I need to make a new memory."

This was the last request I'd expected her to make, but I was starting to wonder if I had the ability to tell her no to anything she asked.

"Okay," I replied, releasing her.

When she stepped back, I pushed Patrick's chair out of the way, ignoring the fact that he rolled into a wall, and cleared off the space in front of his desk. I quickly lifted Honey up onto the desk and stepped in between her open legs.

"No love making, I want you to fuck me," she demanded, unzipping my pants and pulling my dick out.

I captured her mouth with my own at the same time I plunged my dick inside her, swallowing her moan while my tongue fought with hers in angry passion. The speed I set was from zero to a hundred, but her pussy took the punishment with pleasure, evidenced by the wet smacking sound of finger licking goodness. My dick throbbed in rhythm to the beat of her, and even though I knew the danger in that, I kept right on pounding.

"H-harder!" she demanded, breathing raggedly already.

I grabbed a fistful of her hair as I threw my whole body into every stroke I delivered, moving the desk across the room with my force.

"Oh, God!" she moaned loudly, cumming suddenly.

I knew that she still needed more though, and I didn't pause in the slightest. Her eyes burned with the brightness of a thousand suns, but I was too mesmerized to look away as I chased her towards complete fulfillment. Within minutes of her first orgasm, I felt her pussy pulling at me, grabbing me with a fierce possession and need that let me know what was next.

"Oh—"

"Fuck!" I exclaimed, diving inside her as swiftly as I could.

When we came together, it felt like a pipe had burst between us, leaving us both drenched but very much satisfied.

"Was that what-what you had in mind?" I asked, holding on to her tightly.

"N-no, that-that was better," she admitted, chuckling.

When I looked into her eyes, I could see the woman I'd come to know in the past few days, but I knew those demons were just out of sight in the shadows.

"You good?" I asked.

"You make me better," she replied, kissing me tenderly.

"Right back at you, so what do you say we finish up this business?"

"As long as you've got your dick in me, I ain't doing nothing except this," she replied, moving slowly on the object of her desire.

"Mmm, I'd love to do more of this, but I can think of several better locations."

"Okay, fine, but I'm cashing that raincheck," she said, biting my lip before pushing me backwards gently.

I was able to hide the fact that she gave me chills, but I know the smile on my face was like a light in the darkness. After putting my dick away, I turned around to find Father Brennan staring at us in wide-eyed disbelief.

"Sorry, Father, but the little lady gets what she wants. Let's get back to you though, shall we?" I suggested, picking up the shears off his desk and moving towards him purposefully.

"Honey, while I tend to Patrick, can you please clean our DNA off that desk?" I asked, over my shoulder.

"Yes, daddy."

Isn't she amazing?" I asked, putting Patrick's thumb in between the blades and severing it.

By the time I'd removed the remainder of his ten digits, I could tell that he was losing so much blood that not even another shot of adrenaline was gonna keep him focused.

"Well, Father, the good news is that we're almost done, but the bad news is that it only gets worse from here," I said truthfully.

"I'm finished with the desk and I repacked the bag," Honey said, coming up beside me.

"Did you get the money?"

"You should know by now momma don't leave no money on the table," she replied, smiling.

"Didn't I tell you she was amazing, Father?"

"Aww, you mean that, Dollar?" she asked.

"You should know by now that I don't say anything that I don't mean."

I could tell by the look in her eyes that if we didn't stay focused, she was gonna end up getting her screws knocked loose one more time in the here and now. I was tempted, but we both knew there would be other people in the church soon.

"You wanna do the honors?" I asked, passing her the shears.

"He's such a gentleman, Father," she said, smiling genuinely while accepting my gift.

Without hesitation, she unzipped Patrick's pants, pulled his dick out and fit it right in between the blades. The bulge in his eyes was comical, but I kept a straight face.

"I'm positive you won't need this where you're going, Father. I'm gonna warn you, you might feel a little pinch," she said, closing the blades with a vicious squeeze of her hand.

His muffled scream lasted for about ten seconds and then he was out cold.

"Well, that was anti-climactic," she said, frowning.

"The body can only take so much, sweetheart. Why don't you take the bag to the car while I clean up?"

I took the shears back from her and gave her a quick kiss. Once she left, I removed the ball gag, cut the zip ties, and put those things in my pocket. Then I gathered the late Father Brennan's fingers and dick off the floor and sat them on top of his desk. A quick check of his pulse told me he was now trying to plead his case outside the gates of heaven, which meant I could get on with the last piece of business. I carefully pried his mouth open, cut his tongue out and added it to the pile on his desk. A thorough look around the room revealed that I hadn't missed anything, and after tucking the sheers out of sight, I strolled outside to find Honey waiting behind the wheel of the car.

"How about we get some lunch?" I suggested.

"Actually, I had something a little different in mind."

The smile lighting up her face wasn't exactly sexual, but it was promising excitement, nonetheless.

"Let's get rid of all the evidence first," I said, climbing in the passenger seat.

"Sounds like a plan."

We drove around the city disposing of things here and there, until nothing remained of our time with the not-so-holy Father Brennan. Our last stop left me confused though.

"Why are we back at the courthouse?" I asked.

"Well, I was thinking that we went through a lot of work to get that marriage license to cover all of our bases back there. It would be crazy not to use it."

"You-you mean you wanna get married?" I asked.

"Well, since you asked, yeah, I do."

# Chapter 6

"Tabitha Nikole Dewhit, do you take Malcolm David Joyner to be your lawfully wedded husband, to have and to hold, to love, honor and cherish, for richer or poorer, in sickness and in health, for as long as you both shall live?" the justice of the peace asked.

I'd thought this would probably be the moment that reality set in and Honey realized just how crazy this shit was, but her eyes were still blazing with the same unwavering determination.

"I do," she replied eagerly.

As I listened to the judge repeat the same question to me, I wondered how in the hell I'd landed myself in this exact spot with this woman. I mean, we'd known each other for a little more than seventy-two hours, and now we were exchanging vows? This surpassed the definition of crazy! So, why didn't it feel wrong? Not only did it not feel wrong, it made sense on a level that went beyond what words could explain, and the proof of that was in my next two words.

"I do."

"Then by the powers bestowed upon me by the great state of Illinois, I now pronounce you husband and wife. You may kiss the bride," the justice of the peace said, taking a step back.

I pulled her to me and brought our tongues together like the last dance before the club closed. It could've been just my imagination, but I could've sworn that her lips were softer and she tasted sweeter than I remembered.

"All you two have to do is file this with that lady over there, and you're free to live happily ever after," the judge said, handing me the signed marriage certificate, and pointed out the proper clerk.

I took the paper from his hand and led Honey two counters over. Once I'd handed the clerk our marriage certificate, I went right back to communicating with my wife mouth-to-mouth. It was like we'd never kissed anyone else before this moment, like it was always meant to be our lips joined from the beginning of time. We were kissing from our souls.

"You two are good to go," the clerk said, five minutes later.

I took the papers she handed me and we strolled out into the afternoon sun, arm in arm.

"Did that really just happen?" I asked, once we were back in the car.

"You see the ring, don't you?" she replied, flashing me the red plastic from the ring pop I'd bought her.

I looked down at the matching blue one on my finger.

"So, we seriously just got married?"

"Despite the fact that you didn't use your real name, yes we just got married, and I take my vows serious," she replied, starting the car and pulling off.

"Wow," I said slowly.

"You're not having regrets, are you?"

"No, actually I'm not. I can't put into words why it makes sense, but I feel like us being together is bigger than any conscious decision we could make," I replied.

"We're soulmates, it's okay, you can say it."

"I'm not arguing with you, I'm just amazed that all this is happening so fast, I mean there's still so much we don't know about each other," I said.

"Oh, you know plenty about me, but it's like trying to get the nuclear codes when it comes to you telling me about yourself."

"I was taught to listen more than speak," I replied, smiling at the blank look she levelled at me.

"Yeah, well you're a married man now, which means you have no secrets from me. We'll start with something easy, what the hell is your real name?"

Considering everything we'd gone through in the last few days, I had to laugh at the fact that this was her first question.

"You didn't hear the judge, sweetheart? My name is Malcolm David Joyner."

"Right, and you're really from Biloxi, Mississippi too," she replied, hitting me playfully.

"I'll tell you what, let's pick up some food and go back to the motel, and we'll talk there."

"Oh, we're doing more than talk," she said, smiling in a naughty way.

"Indeed."

We got a couple of steak and cheese subs from Uno's, and then we went back to the Motel 6. When we got to our room, I handed her the food, picked her up and carried her across the threshold.

"Aren't you a romantic," she said, kissing me.

"I try."

"That's good because I've never really had a guy give me the romance I crave, and I'm tired of that shit," she stated firmly.

"No worries, I got you now and I know what I'm doing."

"Mmm, well before you show me, I need you to put me down so I can make a quick call," she said.

I put her on her feet, closed the door, and took the bag of food over to the bed. The fact that she took her phone with her into the bathroom with her piqued my curiosity, but I let it go in favor of handling business with my sub and steak fries. By the time she'd come out ten minutes later, my meal was gone, and I was eyeing her food like a god that didn't know no better. That was, until I saw her standing in the bathroom doorway. Naked.

"That must've been a hell of a phone call," I said.

"It was interesting to say the least."

Her walk towards me was effortlessly sexy, and now what I was focused on eating tasted way better than any food ever made.

"Do I wanna know about this interesting call?" I asked, pulling her into my lap.

When she looked at me, I expected to find her eyes full of desire, but instead they were bright with unshed tears. The only reason that I didn't panic was because there was no sadness anywhere that I could see.

"I called my mom to tell her I'd gotten married, and the first thing she said was, '*He* promised to protect you.' Naturally, I was confused, so I asked her who *he* was and to my surprise, she said *your* name. You promised to protect me, Dollar?"

"I did."

"Why?" she asked, genuinely curious.

"Because I'm like no other man you've ever been with. Because I recognize your worth and what you deserve, and I won't give you less. Because you're the only woman I've ever been my complete self around. Maybe my soul recognized its counterpart in you before I could put it into words, but for whatever reason, I made your mom that promise and I mean to keep it," I replied sincerely.

Her smile through the tears sliding down her cheeks was a beautiful sight to behold, and her kiss held the promises of a lifetime.

"What's your real name?" she asked, pulling back suddenly.

I laughed because she was tenacious.

"No one alive knows my real name…but clearly you're not just anyone. The name on my original birth certificate is Dameian Morgan."

"Dameian Morgan…I can see that. Don't worry, I'll still call you Dollar, except for when you're fucking me good," she replied smiling.

For the next two hours, I made her keep that promise as we put every inch of the motel room to good use, finally collapsing in a sweaty heap on the foot of the bed.

"P-promise me it'll al-always be like this," she pointed, holding onto me.

"I promise," I replied, sucking in as much oxygen as I could.

After a few minutes, she had enough energy to sit up and grab her now-cold food.

"Tell me something, how do you know who needs killing?" she asked curiously.

"My accountant handles all the jobs and she sends me the information."

"She?" Honey asked, biting into her sub.

"No, she's never even seen the dick."

"It's a beautiful sight, but I'm not mad that she ain't seen it. So, do you have like a set price for what you do?" she asked.

"It really depends on the situation and how difficult it is. Sometimes, I do pro bono work, like Father Brennan," I replied.

My response made her laugh.

"A killer who does pro bono work, now that's got to be a first."

"Sometimes a muthafucka needs killing more than I need money. Father Brennan lost his life for one dollar," I said seriously.

"One dollar? As in one hundred pennies?"

"Ten dimes, twenty nickels, four quarters, however you want to add it up. I still took that job for *one* dollar," I repeated.

"Hmm."

I didn't exactly know what that meant because I hadn't been around her long enough to learn what her non-verbal grunting meant, but she didn't look like she disappeared.

"So, tell me who Malcolm David Joyner is, since I'm now married to him," she said, passing me the other half of her sub.

"Malcolm is a thirty-seven-year-old investment banker. Never been in trouble, pays his taxes and he owns a bit of land in Mississippi."

"Sounds a little stuffy to be one of your aliases," she replied smiling.

"The point is to create an alias that's completely different from who you really are, that way you're less likely to break character," I said.

"Ah, I see. So, as Mrs. Joyner, am I expected to be a southern belle, at home raising your children?"

"Do you want more kids?" I asked.

"I don't know. I don't know if I can have any more honestly, but I guess we'll find out if I ever miss a period. Do you have any kids?"

"No," I replied shortly.

"Well, do you want any?"

"I didn't think I did until I met you," I replied truthfully.

I could tell that what I said had touched her, but she managed not to do the girl thing and cry.

"So, do you love me?" she asked, smiling.

"As far as I can tell, that's what this feeling is you've created in me."

"When you're one hundred percent sure, I expect you to tell me. And I'll do the same," she said.

"Okay."

For a moment neither of us said anything, and then we burst out laughing.

"Oh, you'll say it first," she vowed.

"We'll see, wife."

"So, what's next?" she asked, finishing off her sandwich.

"That's a good question," I said, getting up so I could get my phone out of my pants.

I quickly dialed the necessary number and listened to it ring twice.

"It's me. It's done," I said.

"You ready for another one?"

"Hold on a second," I said, putting my hand over the phone.

"Do you wanna go on a honeymoon?" I asked my new bride.

"Where would we go?"

"Wherever you want to go, sweetheart," I replied.

"Okay," she said excitedly.

I smiled as I turned my attention back to my phone call.

"Nah, I'm not ready for another one, I'm gonna need a week," I said.

"A week? Why, are you hurt?"

"No, I'm going on my honeymoon," I replied.

"Stop joking, nigga, I'm being serious."

"I *am* being serious," I insisted.

"A honeymoon? When the fuck did you get married?" she asked, shocked.

"A few hours ago."

"You're full of shit, Dollar."

"Baby, say hello to my sister, Aubrey," I said, turning the phone towards her.

"Hi, sister Aubrey!"

"Your crazy ass really got married? To who? Where'd you meet her? How long have you known her?"

"Damn, you need to breathe in between those questions because I know your ass is red in the face right now," I said, laughing.

"Fuck you, smartass. I'm just too fucked up with you right now. I mean, I ain't even heard you mention that you was fucking with no one, so all of this sounds like some impulsive shit, and the Dollar I know is never impulsive."

"I know, right, but you know I trust my instincts though," I said, winking at Honey.

"You can at least tell me her name."

"Her name is Honey. Now, if you don't mind, I've got things to do but I'll be in touch," I replied, hanging up.

"Sounds like she didn't take it too well," Honey said.

"She's just shocked by the suddenness of it all, especially because I don't make impulsive decisions."

"But I like your impulsive side," she said, smiling wickedly.

"You're just saying that because I ate your ass earlier," I replied, laughing.

"Bae, when you did that? Whew! I get the shivers just thinking about it."

"Don't worry, it wasn't a one-time thing, you might even get more of that action on our honeymoon if you tell me where you wanna go," I said.

"I'll tell you, but you gotta promise not to laugh," she replied, coming to stand in front of me.

"Okay."

"Promise me, Dollar."

"I promise," I said, raising my right hand.

"Okay, so I've always wanted to go on one of those cheesy couples' cruises. You know the kind that have things for couples to do, and the bed is shaped like a heart and shit?"

I could feel the immediate twitching in my cheeks, but I fought to keep a straight face with everything in me.

"A-a couples' cruise," I said, clearing my throat.

"Yeah."

The look on her face was to earnest and too sweet for me to do anything except nod my head yes.

"You make the arrangements while I take care of something else," I said, giving her a quick kiss before putting my clothes on.

"Where are you going?" she asked.

"Just out front, don't worry."

I stepped outside and dialed a number from memory that I hadn't used in a while.

"Who is this?" a voice asked, three rings later.

"Dollar."

"Hold on," the voice said.

I heard movement and some rustling, and then her voice came over the line.

"Somebody must be playing on my phone, because the only Dollar I know is dead and gone."

"Not yet, I'm still here, Brianca."

"Isn't that interesting. So, to what do I owe the pleasure of your attention after all this time?" she asked.

The way the word pleasure rolled off her tongue sent my mind racing into a past that was better left forgotten. Brianca and I had met when my path crossed with her dude at the time, an up and coming hustler named Sincere. He was a friend of a friend, and one night we'd all ended up at the same party on the north side of the Chi. Everybody had been having a good time, but it quickly became apparent that Sincere couldn't hold his liquor, and when he saw me dancing with his girl, shit got ugly in a hurry. There were too many people there for me to kill him, but I did beat his muthafuckin' ass for stepping to me sideways. That effectively ended that night of partying, but at two am, I got a text asking me to meet. I was suspicious, but more so curious, so I'd met the five foot five, one-hundred-and-sixty-pound, thick, dark-skinned chick with the chocolate eyes at the Burger King. She showed up with a black eye and a swollen lip, but she wasn't asking me to deal with the nigga who'd done that to her. Her purpose for meeting me was because she figured if she went through all that for just dancing, then she should've just got some dick instead. So, I gave her what she wanted and from then on, she knew who to call when she wanted it. Of course, it didn't take long before she wanted more than dick and that's when things got more than complicated. We hadn't ended on bad terms though.

"I'm calling because I happen to be in your area, and I just came back from Atlanta seeing the Falcons play," I said.

"The Falcons, huh? How much did they win by?"

"Only seven, but the point spread was twenty-three to cover," I replied.

"I can dig it. Well, you know where I'm at, so why don't you come on through," she suggested.

"I'm on my way," I said, hanging up.

I went back into the motel room to tell Honey what the play was, but when I saw her on the phone, I decided to go ahead and get everything together I needed.

"Are we going somewhere?" she asked, hanging up the phone.

"I got a buyer for the coke, so the only thing we'll be travelling with is money."

"How much?" she asked.

"Twenty-three dollars a key, all seven keys."

"Okay, well I'm going with you," she said, putting her clothes on.

"Bae, I'll be right back, I'm just going to meet an old friend," I replied, putting the last brick in the bag, and zipping it.

"That sounds like it's a female you used to fuck, and if it is that's okay because I'm not insecure. I would like to point out that it was you who said that friends become enemies at a moment's notice."

"I know what I said, but this situation is different. I have no interest in who I'm meeting, other than to conduct business, but her seeing you could complicate matters, and I'd hate to have to kiss her because she's Vice Lord," I said.

"Vice Lord?" Honey asked, narrowing her eyes and looking at me closely.

I could tell right away that she was familiar with the gang, but I'd have to hear that story later.

"Yeah, Vice Lord, Four Corner Hustler to be exact," I replied, pulling out my phone and calling an Uber.

"How long do you think you'll be gone?"

"It shouldn't take more than an hour. Is everything ready for our trip?" I asked.

"There's a ship leaving in three days, but that means we've gotta go back to Florida."

"Good thing I haven't made arrangements to get rid of the Chevy yet, which means we'll be driving back through Alabama. Are we stopping to visit my mother-in-law?" I asked.

"Let me think about that," she replied hesitantly.

The sound of a horn honking meant my ride was outside.

"I'll be back soon," I said, kissing her before grabbing the duffle bag, and heading for the door.

"Wait," she said, going to the bed and pulling my .45 from under the pillow.

"Just in case," she said, handing it to me.

I smiled as I tucked it into my pants at the small of my back, and then I walked out. Thirty minutes later, I was dropped off in the projects, and I immediately spotted Brianca sitting out in front of one of the four buildings that she had control over. I could see her smiling already, and she looked the same as she had ten years ago. Suddenly, I felt something knock me off my feet and send me face first into the broken asphalt. By the time the thunder reached my ears, I was coughing up blood and I knew I'd been shot. I could see Brianca walking towards me, but before she got to me, she picked up the duffle bag that flew from my grip.

"Sorry, Dollar, it's nothing personal. Just business."

## Chapter 7
### Two days later

I didn't have to open my eyes to know where I was, and how I'd gotten here was as much a part of my conscious thoughts as it had probably been my subconscious during whatever amount of time had passed. The reoccurring question that this knowledge brought was, *why*? Why had karma chosen that woman with that smile to come and collect the debt that I owed? At this point, the why of the situation would've seemed like a trivial matter to anyone else, but I'd always thought that when it was my time to die, I'd know why that particular person was killing me. The shit Brianca pulled made no sense, even with our complicated history.

"I'm sorry, miss, you can't be in that bed."

"First of all, it's *Mrs.* as in Mrs. Joyner. You here filling in for the regular nurse who called in sick, right?" Honey asked.

"Uh, y-yes, but—"

"Do you know how I know that? Because that nurse tried the same shit that you're about to, and I had to take her outside for a woman-to-woman chat. Do you and I need to go have a conversation?" Honey asked sweetly.

"No, I-I just—"

"You were just about to express your understanding for my need to be by my husband's side as he recovers form massive surgery due to being shot, right? Well, Nurse Tammy Lynn, I really appreciate your understanding, and I'll be sure to inform my husband of how helpful you were when he wakes up," Honey said.

"O-okay. Just use the call button if you need anything."

"Sure thing," Honey replied sweetly.

I wanted to laugh, but I had no illusions about how much that would hurt.

"That's gangsta," I whispered.

"Glad you approve," Honey said, laying her head back on my shoulder.

"Where are we?"

"If you'd open your eyes, you would see that we're in a hospital," she replied.

I could hear the edge in her voice, but given how badly I'd misread the situation I knew she had every right to be mad.

"I know we're in a hospital, but it's not loud enough to be Cook County, so where are we?" I repeated.

"I brought you home to Biloxi."

"Hearing this made my eyes snap open and had me looking around for signs that she was bullshitting, but I found nothing to confirm or deny what she'd said.

"There's no way we're in Mississippi, how long was I out?" I asked.

"It's been two days since you made me your wife, and tried to make me your widow. You had to be sedated because the bullet had to be removed from your lung, and when I informed the doctor that I wanted to transport you immediately, he agreed to keep you unconscious."

"How did you even know I was in the hospital or that I'd been shot?" I asked, confused.

"*I'm* the one who got you to the hospital after I *saw you* get shot."

"Huh? That would mean—"

"That would mean I followed you, and it's a good thing for both of us that I did, or you'd be another unidentified body in the Chicago morgue. I'd pulled into the neighborhood just in time to see you hit the ground, and my instincts kicked in," she said.

"What exactly does that mean?"

"That means I didn't even waste time getting out of the car before I started shooting at the bitch who grabbed the duffle bag. I was able to get you in the car and get you to the hospital, and once I found out you'd live, I knew there was no way we could stay in Chicago," she replied.

"Did you get her?"

"No, and as badly as I wanted to chase her muthafuckin' ass, it was more important to take care of you," she replied, snuggling closer to me.

Knowing that she'd put her life on the line for me had me at a loss for words. No one had done that before, but this beautiful stranger had done it without hesitation or thought to her own safety.

"That's gangsta," I said.

"What can I say, you're rubbing off on me."

"Speaking of rubbing, I know just how soft your body is, so what do you have hard pressed against my leg?" I asked.

"Your .45, just in case Chicago's troubles travelled down here. I got no problem shooting it out right here."

"I love you," I blurted out.

"I love you too. And I told you that you'd say it first," she replied, chuckling.

"I don't mind because I meant it. I've never known anyone like you, but I love you."

"Right back at you, but I need to tell you something. The next time you put yourself in harm's way unnecessarily, I'ma fuck you up and that's real talk," she said, looking at me.

"I understand, and I should've listened to you. I really didn't expect that though, and I still don't know why she played me like that."

"I'm sure you'll get that answer sooner or later, but for now we need to focus on your healing," she replied sternly.

"Okay, but I don't do hospitals, especially because the police like to ask questions of gunshot victims."

"The cops already did their questioning in Chicago. I told them you were in the projects looking at properties to tear down and rebuild for the investment group you represent, and I believed your shooting was you being mistaken for a cop. Or, it was an attempted robbery gone wrong. Either way, the last thing the city of Chicago needed was public scrutiny over the shooting of an out of town businessman, and the last thing you would want is for the deal to fall apart. So the police agreed to investigate quietly, and assist me in any way they could with getting you safely back to Mississippi," she concluded.

"You really are amazing, you know that?" I asked, impressed by how quickly she thought on her feet.

"I'm glad you recognize that because from now on, whatever has to be done we do it together, unless it's just completely impossible. I will respect that I can't go along for every business trip, but I won't be ignored or left in the dark. Agreed?"

"Agreed," I replied, smiling.

"Glad we could have this conversation. So, if I spring you from the hospital, where exactly would I be taking you?"

"I told you we own a little land down here, and there's a nice house we can hold up in. That's only if you're up to taking care of me, because we can hire a nurse—"

"I did mention there will be *no* threesomes in this relationship, right?" she asked, grabbing my dick under the covers.

"Baby, I thought you liked women."

"I do, I love women, especially the ones that don't get the dick from my husband. I don't know what that bitch in Chicago's problem was, but I guarantee that not getting your loving anymore is at the root of it. So, if it's all the same to you, I'll be the only female to fuck you, suck you, and nurse you back to health," she said seriously.

"I'm too smart to argue."

"That's music to my ears, now just lay right here while I go get your doctor," she ordered, kissing me quickly.

She climbed gingerly from the bed to prevent a lot of movement, and she left me my gun under the blanket, which made me smile at her thoughtfulness. That smile quickly faded though as I thought about how close I'd come to never being able to enjoy my wedded bliss. I knew taking on Brianca meant taking on the people's nation, but there was no way I could allow her treachery to go unpunished. I just had to figure out when I wanted to do it and how, because it would require patience on my part in order to cause the most damage with the least amount of effort.

"Ah, Mr. Joyner, it's good to see you're awake. I'm Dr. Tyne. How are you feeling?"

"Is that a trick question? I feel like I had some hot shit in my chest that wasn't supposed to be there," I replied, looking at the tall, gray-haired white man like he was crazy.

"That's understandable. A twenty-two can do more damage to your body than a forty-five slug sometimes. The good news is that the operation they performed in Chicago got the bullet out without leaving any fragments behind, and no infection had set in. although advances in medicine help people to recuperate faster from things like surgery and bullet wounds, I still think a few more days in the hospital would be appropriate."

"Ain't happening," I said shortly.

'I'm sure he was opening his mouth to give me some good reasons why it would be to my benefit to stay in the hospital, but Honey didn't let him get a word out.

"Doc, it ain't happening. My husband is a very determined man, and I'm like minded, so let's not waste time arguing when you could be taking care of the prescriptions and discharge paperwork."

The doctor looked at her and then looked at me, and I could tell he understood what was in his best interest.

"I'll get right on that," he said, retreating the way that he'd come.

"Shall we get you dressed?" Honey asked, smiling.

"Only if you don't try no funny business because you know I'm physically incapable right now."

"I'll be on my best behavior," she replied, raising her right hand and crossing her fingers.

When I laughed, I felt exactly how close I'd come to dying because the pain in my chest was still excruciating. I was scared to take a full breath because when I did, it felt like I'd swallowed the sun. It was a full thirty minutes later before I was dressed, and my clothes were already sticking to me because of how much I was sweating.

"You sure you don't wanna stay a few more days?" Honey asked, concern clouding her eyes.

"Are you doubting your ability to take care of me now?"

"No, I got you, I just don't like seeing you in pain," she replied.

"Pain is good, it's motivation, and it'll keep me focused."

"I can only trust your opinion, but I'm telling now if shit gets too bad, you're bringing your ass back to the hospital," she said.

Before I could respond, she left the room again. As fast as my injury would allow, I tucked my gun under my shirt in my jeans, and then proceeded to disconnect the needle from the IV and collect anything with my blood on it that I could find. By the time Honey returned, I felt like I'd done all I could to leave as little of myself behind as possible.

"I got your prescriptions, and you've been discharged."

"I want you to take the sheets and blankets off the bed, and find a bag to put them in because they're going with us. Then I want you to wipe everything down in here that you or I touched," I said.

Once she helped me into a chair, she got to work, moving with speed and efficiency. I watched her close to make sure that she didn't miss anything, but she took my initial instructions to heart and cleaned the room more thoroughly than any janitor could. As badly as I didn't want to use a wheelchair, I knew that I had to. But instead of taking it back inside once she'd gotten me to the car, she folded that muthafucka up and put it in the trunk.

"It was risky for you to drive all the way down here," I said, noticing the duffle bags in the back of the Bonneville.

"Now didn't seem like a particularly good time to get rid of the guns we have, so it was worth the risk. Where are we going?"

I gave her directions to my house, and we were on the move. An hour later, we arrived and I could tell by the look she was giving me, she had questions.

"What?" I asked.

"I believe your exact words were that you had a *nice* house and a *little* land."

"Okay, so what's the problem?" I asked, smiling.

"Dollar, this is an old plantation house, which means all the land I see around us is part of this estate. That makes your description just a little misleading, don't you think?"

"So, what's the problem?" I repeated, laughing at her exasperated expression.

"Yeah, I can tell that we're gonna have to have a *long* talk about what full disclosure means," she replied, getting out of the car and coming around to my side.

It had been awhile since I'd been out here, but it was a place I liked to come because it was quiet. The neighbors were so far away, we'd never had a reason to meet. Therefore, no one bothered me out here. When I'd first bought the house about eight years back, I'd had it restored to what it would've looked like in the seventeen hundred's, while adding the necessary touches of modernization. I'd been smart about it though, I didn't hire a bunch of outside contractors to come in and do the work, I'd used all local people. That way the money stayed in the community, they felt like they were a part of my home and its history, and I was accepted as one of them because I made the decision to do the right thing. Dollar was a cold-blooded killer, but Malcolm Joyner was a pillar of the community who would have a street named after him one day.

"How many bedrooms?" Honey asked, helping me towards the house.

"Twelve bedrooms, six upstairs and six downstairs. Five bathrooms, a gaming room, a study, and a library. Double wraparound porches, top and bottom, and there's even a wine cellar. I updated all the appliances in the kitchen, added indoor plumbing, and the other creative comforts to live good in this century."

"Sounds like heaven. Did I tell you that I can cook?" she asked.

"No, you neglected that bit of information. I doubt that there's any food here other than canned goods, so you'll have to go shopping. Take the Lincoln in the garage, Mrs. Joyner can't be seen around town pushing a hoopty," I replied, smiling at her.

"Whatever you say, dear. So, do you got a key to get in this place or what?"

"It's under the third floorboard," I said, nodding towards the hiding spot.

Despite having both porches completely redone I used distressed wood to give it an aged look, so a broken or rotted-looking board wouldn't draw anyone's attention. Honey grabbed the key, unlocked the door, and helped me inside. As soon as we crossed the threshold I heard the noise, and I could tell by the look on Honey's face that I wasn't imagining what I was hearing.

"Is someone house sitting?" Honey whispered.

I shook my head no, while pulling my pistol and pointing towards the direction the sounds were coming from. The closer we got, the more recognizable the noises became, and I had a feeling I knew who I would find in my house. We crept slowly around the corner of the open bedroom door, finding a broad-shouldered black dude asshole naked, fucking the shit out of a female. I didn't need to see the female's face because I knew who she was.

"I'm gonna have to kindly ask you to step out of the pussy and leave," I said calmly.

My voice startled the man, but only enough to make him look back, not pull out.

"Who-who the fuck are you?" he asked.

"The owner of this house," I replied.

“Oh shit,” the girl beneath him mumbled.

“Well, come back later, because—”

Just for him being too stupid to follow instructions, I pulled the trigger and planted his brains above the bed’s headboard.

“Jesus Christ, did you have to shoot him?” the naked girl asked, scrambling from the bed.

“Yep,” I replied.

“I see you still ain’t changed, huh, Dad?”

# Chapter 8

"I'm sorry, did she just call you *Dad*?" Honey asked, looking at me like I had *a lot* of explaining to do.

"She did, but it's not meant as advertised," I replied.

"Oh yes it is, *Dad,* because we both know you've been dying to run my life since I was born!"

"Dollar, please make some sense out of this," Honey requested.

"This is Iree, my sister. I know the light skin and curly hair throws off the resemblance, but we're related," I said.

"Oh no, I can see it in her face. Especially because she's pissed," Honey replied.

"You damn right I'm pissed! He *always* does this shit! It doesn't matter what guy I'm with or how much I love him, my brother step-daddy finds a reason to kill him."

"So, let me get this straight, you bring a nigga into *my* house and decide to fuck him, and I'm the bad guy for shooting him?" I asked.

"You didn't *have* to shoot him, you could've been civilized and—"

"He did ask him to step out of the pussy and leave," Honey pointed out.

"Do you stop before you get your nut?" Iree countered.

"We're grown," I said.

"Wait, she's not grown?" Honey asked, looking Iree over from head to toe.

"Oh she may have the body of an adult, but she's sixteen years old," I replied.

"*Wow*, I was lusting over some jail bait," Honey said, shaking her head.

Her comment made Iree smile, which only served to piss me off more.

"Put some fucking clothes on and explain why you're in my house," I demanded.

"I'm in your house because you *told* me I could be," she replied, with her hands on her hips and her neck rolling.

"You're really sixteen though?" Honey asked, still in disbelief.

"I told you that you could come here in the case of an emergency and if *I* was here," I said.

"Yeah, well, you're never here. Plus, me and my mom were fighting and I needed a break."

"Oh yeah, you're definitely sixteen," Honey said, nodding her head.

This time Iree gave her a nasty look, instead of a smile.

"How long have you been here?" I asked.

"A couple weeks," she replied vaguely.

"Does your mom know you're here?" I asked.

"Well, not exactly because—"

"Get out," I demanded.

"Dollar, will you just *listen* to me—"

"Nope. Put your clothes on, get your shit and get out. Go back to Alabama," I said.

"You're from Alabama?" Honey asked.

"Babe, not now," I said, trying to focus on solving the immediate problem.

"No, I'm not leaving, and you can't make me," Iree replied suddenly, crossing her arms over her chest.

Ordinarily, I had all the patience in the world with her because I did love her and treat her like my daughter, but she was seriously picking the wrong day to fuck with me.

"Iree, get dressed, and *get out*," I said forcefully.

"Dollar, *fuck you*," she replied, smiling.

"Honey, give me your phone," I said, holding my hand out.

"Who you gonna call, *Ghostbusters*? I *know* you ain't calling the cops, not with that warm body on the floor over there," Iree taunted.

"Technically, that's a justifiable homicide because that's *clearly* a grown ass man, fucking an underage girl, in his house," Honey pointed out, passing me her phone.

I dialed a number quickly and waited impatiently for it to be answered.

"Leigha, do you know where your daughter is?" I asked.

"No, but I'm assuming that you do if you're calling me."

"Yeah, she's with me. She had a little accident, but she's fine. Are you cool with her staying with me for a little while?" I asked.

"Keep her," Leigha replied, hanging up.

I passed the phone back to Honey.

"Baby, that was nice of you," Honey said.

"Yeah, Dollar, I appreciate you—"

Whatever she was gonna say was forgotten as pain took ahold of all her senses, forcing her to scream as she lay on the ground clutching her right leg and the bullet hole in it.

"You-you fucking *shot me*!" she yelled through her tears.

"Did you really just shoot your sister?" Honey asked, shocked.

"You mean my *daughter*? Yeah, I did that," I replied, moving slowly towards her until I was standing over her.

"That's *beyond* gangsta," Honey said, shaking her head.

"Now, since you were so intent in staying here I gave you a reason, and your mom knows where you are. It's a win-win," I said.

"You-you *shot* me," she replied, crying harder.

"Do you want me to do it again?" I asked calmly.

"No! Don't!"

"Then act accordingly," I replied, turning around and slowly making my way back towards Honey.

"You'll find everything you need to clean and bandage her wound in the first aid kit in the bathroom across the hall. If you don't mind," I said, kissing her softly.

"I'll take care of her, as soon as I get you somewhere where you can lay down," she replied, helping me back out of the room.

She took me two doors down to another spare bedroom, and helped me lay down.

"Just rest and I'll take care of everything," she reassured me.

The exhaustion I felt went bone deep, and it wasn't long after my head touched the pillow that my eyes refused to stay open. My dreams started off peacefully of Brianca and I back in the day, laughing, fucking, even fighting sometimes because the make-up sex was worth it. Those images quickly changed to her standing over me, pointing a gun at my head while telling me it was just business. The sound of the gun going off snatched me from my sleep, and the pain in my chest kept me awake. For a moment, Honey standing in front of me with her hands straight up in the air made no sense, but then I saw the moonlight illuminating the gun outstretched in my hand.

"You okay?" Honey asked softly.

"Yeah," I replied, letting my arm drop and laying back down.

I felt her weight on the bed and then she was curled up against me.

"I know I stink," I said.

"So?"

"What time is it?" I asked.

"A little after eight pm. You slept for a while, but you obviously needed that rest," she replied.

"I smell food."

"I cooked pasta and sausage, my grandma's secret recipe from the old country," she said.

"How is Iree?"

"She'll live, but she's pissed at you. Actually, I think she's more hurt than anything, because she never thought that side of you would come to light towards her. She loves you, Dollar."

"I love her too, but she drives me crazy sometimes," I said honestly.

"It's our kid's job to drive us crazy, and despite you two being siblings, she really does look at you like her father."

"Seems like you two had a long talk," I commented.

"Well, if you're not gonna tell me about yourself then someone had to. Don't worry, all your secrets are safe with me," she replied.

I didn't need to look at her to know she was smiling because I could hear it in her voice.

"If I didn't know you could keep a secret, I wouldn't have married you."

"Don't I know it. From what Iree tells me I've gotta be something special, because you swore you were never getting married, after the first disaster you went through," she said.

"I guess you can never say never."

We laid there in silence for a few moments, but I could feel her wanting to talk.

"You wanna know, huh?" I asked.

"I feel like I already do. She hurt you, didn't she?"

"Yeah," I replied shortly.

"I won't."

The feeling of her lacing her fingers with mine after she spoke those simple but powerful words eased the pain in my chest, and not just what I felt as a result of my gunshot wound. I wasn't really the type to deal with the past when it came to emotional situations because I believed in growing and moving on. Sometimes you couldn't plant new seeds until you'd retilled the soil.

"You love me?" I asked.

"I guess that's the best way to describe the feelings that you create in me."

"So, do you think I was wrong for what I did earlier?" I asked.

"Not for shooting dude…and I wouldn't necessarily say you were wrong for how you handled Iree, but it was *definitely* extreme," she replied.

"Where is she?"

"At the table eating. You feel up to making the trip?" she asked.

"You got my back?"

"Always," she replied without hesitation.

I passed her my gun and then I slowly got up out of the bed. My chest still hurt like a muthafucka, but I was confident in taking deep breaths. We made our way out of the bedroom and to the huge dining room table where Iree was sitting with her right leg propped up. I kissed her on the top of the head before sitting down next to her;

"I'll make you a plate," Honey said, leaving us alone.

For a moment I stared at Iree and she did her best to ignore me.

"You're beautiful when you're angry."

"Are you gonna shoot me for that too?" she asked sarcastically.

"No…I'm sorry that I shot you in the first place."

"It hurt," she said softly.

Even as the tear tumbled from her eye and cascaded down her face, I knew she wasn't talking about any physical pain. I'd hurt her emotionally because we were thicker than thieves and closer than most. It never mattered to her how long I disappeared for, because she knew that only death would stop me from coming back to her.

"I love you, Ree-ree," I said, leaning over and kissing her cheek.

"Does that mean I get to shoot you back?" she asked, smiling.

"Relax, you were still fucking a nigga in my house."

"But, I wasn't in your bed though," she pointed out.

The look I gave her let it be known just how pointless her argument was.

"Thank you, baby," I said, accepting my plate of food from Honey.

She sat down across from me with her plate, giving me a wink.

"So, I heard somebody tried to permanently turn your lights off," Iree said.

"Shit happens sometimes," I replied.

"Not to you, I mean, I ain't never known you to get caught slippin'," Iree insisted.

"Who said I was slippin' this time around?" I asked, looking pointedly at my wife.

All she did was smile at me.

"Isn't it kind of obvious that if you walked into an ambush, you were slippin'?" Iree asked slowly.

"You think you're cute, huh?" I asked, looking directly at my wife.

"Shit, I know I'm fine and if I was just two years older, I'd show your old lady which one of us can suck pussy better," Iree replied confidently.

Her statement turned Honey's chuckling into outright laughter, but I suppressed my smile so I wouldn't encourage my sister's bullshit.

"Yeah, whatever, ain't you learned your lesson about thinking with your pussy?" I asked.

There was no witty comeback from Iree, but she stuck her tongue out at me which finally forced me to laugh. We put the serious conversation on hold and just kicked it like any other time we'd shared a meal, with the added bonus of Honey of course. It still hurt like a muthafucka to laugh, but it was impossible not to with these two characters in front of me. A couple times I caught Honey mouthing the words, *I love you*, and I said it right back gladly.

"So how did you two meet because I know that had to be some hell of a story," Iree said.

"I was working," I replied shortly.

"And I'd been waiting for him my whole life," Honey said.

"Aww, that's so sweet. How long have you two been together?" Iree asked.

"Today makes five, doesn't it bae?"

"Yes it does, and it's been magical," Honey replied smiling.

"Dollar, how the hell did you manage to keep her a secret for *five* years?"

"No, no, no it's been five *days*," Honey corrected.

"Magical days," I chimed in.

"Five-five days? You're serious?" Iree asked, shocked.

"I know that probably seems sudden, but when you know, you know," Honey said.

"Five days...well that absolutely settles it. Dollar can suck pussy better than me."

We all burst out laughing as my wife and sister exchanged high-fives. Once we finished eating, Iree excused herself so she could call her mom and make shit right.

"Is there still a body in her room?" I asked.

"No, he's in the trunk of the Bonneville with his big ass. I was cussing your ass out the whole time I was dragging him out there, and while I was cleaning up his brains."

"Thank you, baby, I owe you," I said sincerely.

"Oh, don't think I'm not keeping a running tally because you most definitely will pay what you owe."

"I have no doubts, but it'll be my pleasure to repay you with interest," I promised.

"See, you can't be using that tone or looking at me like that when you know you're not in the condition to give me dick."

"You say that like you need it already, it's only been two days," I said, smiling.

"When you having good sex, two days to go without it is *too damn long*! You hear me?" she asked seriously.

"I hear you, baby. Did you get my medication so we can start this healing process?"

She quickly got up and went back into the kitchen, returning with a pill bottle and a new cell phone.

"I figured you'd need this too," she said.

"Yeah, it's about time to get some answers."

I made sure to take two pain pills first, and then I made my call while Honey was clearing the table.

"It's me."

"My fucking God, Dollar, what the hell happened? I've been getting calls for days saying you were dead," Aubrey said emotionally.

"Who called you?"

"Competitors, old clients too. Word was that the streets of Chiraq swallowed you whole and you were never to be seen or heard from again," she replied.

"Did they say who did it?"

"Some Vice Lord bitch tried to collect on an old bounty, but the nigga who set the price ain't been seen in a while. Dollar, what the fuck is going on?"

"That's what I'm trying to figure out. I thought I was doing business with a friend, and the next thing I know I'm wondering if heaven got a ghetto," I replied honestly.

"That's crazy."

"Tell me about it. Who put the original price on me?" I asked.

"The name I got was Ghost, but you know that could be a million muthafuckas so—"

"Nah, I think I know who it is," I said slowly.

The way the puzzle fit together made sense. Around the time that I'd left Chicago, Sincere had gone missing, but nobody was claiming responsibility and the streets weren't talking. My beef with him had been so old that it was forgotten by everybody. Everybody except Sincere's little brother, Ghost. I'd known back then I was supposed to kill him, but I'd honestly felt like he wasn't worth the bullet. Right now, I could feel why the assessment had been a mistake.

"The Vice Lord is a bitch named Brianca. She used to fuck with a nigga named Sincere, who had a brother named Ghost," I said.

"Oh, I see."

"I'm sure you do. Find out everything you can and get it to me. I'm staying off the radar for a couple weeks to heal up, but I'll check in with you every couple days," I said.

"Okay. Please be safe, you ain't Superman, you know."

"No, but I'm a bad muthafucka," I replied, hanging up.

"You get the answers you were looking for?" Honey asked, bringing me a slice of apple pie.

"You bake too?"

"I do, but this is store bought," she replied.

"You keep this shit up and I'ma marry you again," I said, smiling.

"You promise?"

"*I do*," I stated emphatically.

"I'm down for whatever, you know that. Speaking of which, what's our next move?"

"First, I'm gonna heal up. Then, it's back to killing."

# Chapter 9
## Two weeks later

"It's me. I'm ready," I said.

"Aight, I got two for you. Texas and Florida."

"Yee-haw," I replied, hanging up.

"Did you just say yee-haw?" Honey asked, smirking at me from the chair that she was occupying on the other side of my desk.

"I did. Do you have a problem with that?"

"No, not at all, but I'd love an explanation on when and how you became a cowboy," she replied.

"I told you before that I'm anything or anyone I need to be at any time."

"That's kinda like that old Janet Jackson song, 'Anytime Anyplace,' huh?" she asked.

"Very funny, smartass," I replied, throwing a paperclip at her, while accessing my private email.

My movements were still a little stiff, but I'd healed nicely from my brush with death, and now it was time to get back to being the Grim Reaper. Two weeks of doing nothing except laying around had given me cabin fever severe enough to make me want to crawl out of my skin! I'd tried several times to convince Honey that I was ready to go back to active duty, but she wasn't hearing it, and Iree sided with her of course. It didn't take me long to discover that two vaginas was too many for me to win an argument against. I blamed Beyoncé for putting out that women's anthem, "Who Runs The World."

"Come here, I wanna show you something," I said, sliding my chair a little to the left so that she could move around and see the screen.

"What am I looking at?"

"The target," I replied.

"Wow, that's a lot of information on Mr. Chuck Hillson. You know everything, down to his favorite color."

"You never know what information might prove helpful when you're going after someone. People tend to trust people they have things in common with. Say I bumped into Chuck at Starbucks, had a green sweater on, ordered a double shot espresso, and was mumbling to myself about the Cowboy's football game. There are too many segues into conversation for Chuck not to talk to me, and once he does that, everything else is based on opportunity," I said.

"So, is that your plan for Mr. Hillson?" she asked.

"No, because you see right here where it says the reason he's supposed to die is so his wife can collect on the life insurance? Well, insurance companies tend to drag their feet if a death wasn't accidental or from natural. Murder makes their Spidey sense tingle, so I have to kill him in a way that looks accidental. Father Brennan on the other hand? That killing needed to be loud so that the victims would feel safe and the next muthafucka would think twice."

"So, how are you gonna get rid of Chuck?" she asked.

I studied the dossier in front of me silently for a moment, thinking of and discarding ideas that didn't work, until one slid into place.

"Chuck likes to fish and he likes to be on the water, so what I'll do is have Aubrey send him free weekend passes for a fishing retreat, and make it so they have a short time limit to be used," I said.

"You think that'll work?"

"People love free shit, especially when it has something to do with a favorite hobby. Plus, I'm guessing that since the wife hired me for the job, the marriage is set up where they enjoy spending time apart," I replied.

"So, after you tell Aubrey what you need, what's next?"

"Then I let her know what type of weapons I need, and what kind of transportation. I try to drive what I know will blend in with whatever environment I'm going into, and it's best not to ride with a bunch of guns if I don't have to. Aubrey has people all across the country to supply what we need on short notice, and it's always untraceable," I said.

"Should I be worried that all of this seems fun to me?" she asked, laughing.

"Nah, we both know that you're a beautiful savage."

"A beautiful savage…I like that. It's crazy that you get me the way no one else had!" she said, quickly kissing me before turning her attention back to the screen.

I shot Aubrey an email, telling her what I was gonna need.

"Hopefully, within the next seven days, old Chuck will become the victim of an unfortunate drowning accident," I said.

"So, now what do we do, start packing?"

"Not yet. I accepted two jobs, so now she'll send me the second set of information," I replied.

"Well, while we wait on that I'm gonna make a sandwich. You want one?"

"I could eat," I said.

"Yes, you can," she purred, kissing me passionately.

"It's bad enough I gotta listen to you two fuck like wild animals, but do I actually have to see it too?" Iree asked, limping into my study.

"It would serve your ass right after the way you scared me," I replied.

"And you ain't got no room to talk about how we sound with the way you was carrying on," Honey stated.

"The male ego is fragile, so a little encouragement never hurts," Iree said.

"Sorry, I don't have that problem," Honey replied, kissing me again thoroughly.

"Sure, just rub it in!" Iree said sourly.

When Honey finally turned my mouth loose, I smacked her on the ass like rent was due, which made her giggle as she walked away.

"You're such a hypocrite," Iree said, shaking her head as she sat down across from me.

"Not even close, that's my wife."

"You still having sex, and I know that you were fucking at my age so don't even try to lie," she said.

"You're right, I was, but I was a lot dumber than you too," I admitted.

"So, having sex is dumb now?"

"I didn't say that. As far as I'm concerned, the dumb shit you do starts in between your ears, not in between your legs. Your pussy has value, but if you can't realize that, how the fuck do you expect a nigga to?' I asked seriously.

"I know my pussy has value," she replied defensively.

"Really? So, how long did you know that nigga you was fucking? What was the name his momma gave him? Is anyone gonna miss him now that he's dead and gone?"

"Fuck you, Dollar," she said angrily.

Her attitude made me chuckle.

"The last time you said that I shot you, but I'm not gonna do that this time, I'm just gonna keep it one thousand with you. By no means am I judging you, Iree, because we both know that I'm nobody to judge. You're beautiful, intelligent, funny, and caring, and all of that equates to a good woman, but if you keep doing shit that's gonna make you question your self-worth later on, then you're gonna lose yourself.

What I'm saying is if five years from now, you close your eyes and all you can see is the niggas you've let jump up and down in you, how are you really gonna feel about yourself? Are you gonna see yourself as a beautiful queen, or a woman who had been used until she'd all used up? You control your life, and the answers to those questions."

I could see the weight of my words in the tears in her eyes, but everything I'd said was what she needed to hear. I wouldn't always be around to shoot niggas, and the reality was that I couldn't live her life for her anyway. I could love her though, and I'd always do that. Slowly she got up and made her way around the desk so she could sit in my lap.

"I love you, Dad," she said softly, burying her face in my neck, like she'd done so long ago.

I held her tight while she cried silently. I knew the fact that our father had died when she was younger still haunted her, and was what fed her demons sometimes, but I'd promised to love her through it all. I would keep that promise.

"If I promise to try and do better, can I stay here for a while?" she asked, leaning back so she could look at me.

It was on the tip of my tongue to say of course, but my eyes were momentarily frozen on my laptop. What I saw turned my blood from human to reptilian.

"Dollar…what is it?" Iree asked, following my gaze.

Honey picked that exact moment to walk back into the room with my sandwich.

"Honey, I didn't know you were a Bama fan, and the name Tabitha really doesn't suit you," Iree said, looking from the screen to Honey and back.

"What are you two up to…Dollar wh-what the fuck is that?" Honey asked in a strangled whisper, now looking at the information that had popped on my laptop.

"Ree-Ree, hop up," I said, already reaching for my phone.

"What's going on?" Iree asked, confused, but still moving.

The sound of the phone ringing in my ear was like nails on a chalkboard, but after what seemed like an eternity it was answered.

"Aubrey, the info you sent was incomplete, it doesn't say who or why."

"That's because it was a third-party deal, double-blind, and double your normal fee for rush delivery," she replied.

Everything she'd just said meant that whoever had put a hit on Honey went through extreme measures to keep their identity a secret.

"That's no good, I need all the information, Aubrey."

"I'll see what I can find out, but you know the payment has already been accepted. I don't see what the problem is, it's just some bitch—"

"You don't gotta see what the damn problem is, just find out the info!" I yelled, hanging up the phone.

"Dollar, is this, is this for real?" Honey asked, coming to stand beside me.

"Will somebody tell me what the hell is going on?" Iree asked.

"Baby, I'm gonna fix this, okay? I'm gonna fix it," I vowed, pulling her onto my lap.

"Who-who would wanna kill me?" she asked, disbelief evident in her voice.

"What?" Iree exclaimed.

"Tabitha, look at me, *nobody* is gonna kill you. I will *never* let that happen, baby."

"Never say never," she replied hollowly.

"Ree-Ree, go in my room and look in one of those duffle bags in the closet until you find the weed. I want you to roll the biggest blunt you can and bring it to me," I instructed.

She moved without hesitation, leaving us alone for the moment. I took the sandwich from Honey's hand, put it down and turned her to face me.

"Baby, no matter what, I'm gonna protect you even if I gotta give up my life," I said earnestly.

"I just don't understand who I pissed off that much for them to send you after me."

I wasn't insulted by what she said, because the truth was muthafuckas knew I wasn't picky about who I eliminated, and I always got my man like the IRS. Double the fee for rush delivery meant somebody had spent a quarter of a million dollars, and that meant whoever it was wasn't simply pissed. They were serious.

"You already heard me tell Aubrey to find out who put the contract out, so we just gotta wait until that information comes through," I said.

"But what if, what if in the meantime somebody—"

"Baby, the job has already been accepted by me, so there's no one else coming. Besides, even if they were, they'd have no idea how to find you because you're with me," I assured her.

For a moment it looked like some calm was returning to her face, but then her eyes filled up with tears and her lips started trembling.

"Dollar, my-my family. What if they go after my family?"

There was no way I'd lie to her and say there wasn't a possibility of that happening, because the reality was that would've been my first stop if I was looking for her.

"Call your mom," I instructed, passing her my phone.

I watched her dial the number with shaky fingers, and then listen to it ring on the other end.

"M-Mom, it's me."

I immediately took the phone from her hand.

"Mrs. Dewhit, It's Dollar."

"Is everything okay?" she asked, concerned.

"No, it's not and I need you to listen to me carefully and do exactly what I tell you to do. I want you, your husband and the kids, to get in your car right now and drive to Mississippi. Don't tell anyone you're leaving or where you're going, don't pack a single thing, just get in the car and leave. *Now*," I stated emphatically.

My demand was met with a silence that I knew had a large amount of questions in it, and I was praying this woman didn't start asking them.

"Can you text me the destination?" she finally asked.

"I can do that. As soon as you're on the road, I want you to text this number and I'll send you the address."

"We're on our way," she replied, hanging up.

"Okay, where are the rest of your kids?" I asked Honey.

"My oldest son is overseas in the Army, and my other oldest daughter is on vacation in Italy with her husband."

"Well, your son has better protection than even I can offer, but I want you to call your daughter and tell her to stay where she is," I said, passing her the phone.

She got up from my lap and sat back in the chair she'd occupied earlier, and I turned my attention back to my laptop. I needed to find some type of clue or trail to follow so I could put my hacking skills to work and unmask whoever was pulling these particular strings. I knew that whoever it was, was gonna lose their life and they'd just made sure everyone close to them suffered the same fate. The smell of smoke diverted my attention momentarily as I accepted the blunt that Iree passed my way, but it gave me time to sit back and contemplate.

"Is someone really trying to kill your wife?" Iree asked.

"Who told you to roll your own blunt?" I asked, looking at her standing beside me puffing away.

"Relax, I rolled three, and letting me smoke your weed is the least you could do since you shot me."

"You're just gonna keep milking that, ain't you?" I asked.

"I'd be a fool not to, and you didn't raise no fools. Now answer my question, is this shit real?"

"Yeah, it's real," I replied, fighting not to let the rage that I felt consume me.

"Yo, that's crazy. How they gonna send you to kill your own wife though? Somebody clearly didn't think this through."

"Nah, I'm sure that they'd thought it through. They just didn't realize who they were fucking with," I replied seriously.

"Dollar, she says they don't have enough money to stay for too much longer," Honey said, putting her hand over the phone.

"Tell her to get to the nearest bank and I'll wire them enough money to tour Italy, and then bounce around Europe for a while. Under *no* circumstances are they to come back into the country until we say so," I replied.

She nodded her head and went back to her conversation.

"You know I've never seen you like this with a woman before. I mean, you've protected me my whole life, but I've never seen you like this when it came to someone who wasn't blood," Iree said.

"Our connection is stronger than blood. I can't explain it, I just know that it's real and I'm not about to let *any* muthafucka take it from me."

"Oh, I have no doubt about that. What's your first move?" Iree asked.

"Right now we're making sure that her family is straight. Her parents and her two youngest kids are on their way here, and I expect you to make them feel welcome in my house," I replied seriously.

"I will be the definition of southern hospitality, I promise. How old are her kids?"

"Her son is ten and her daughter's fifteen, and your little ass better not corrupt either of them in any way. Understand?" I asked.

"I would *never*!"

The smile on her face and the blunt in between her lips made it impossible to take her seriously, but at the end of the day I knew she was a good kid.

"Don't make me shoot you again," I said, smiling at her.

"You do that shit again and I'm telling my mom because she'll shoot your ass back."

I didn't argue with the truth in that statement.

"She's headed to the bank now," Honey said, laying my phone on the desk and taking a deep breath.

"Okay. Your parents should be here by nightfall," I replied.

"Dollar, how am I gonna explain this to them, and what the hell am I gonna say to the kids?" she asked.

"The kids will get the new house, new husband, investment banker story, and we'll tell them that we brought them out here so we could get acquainted. We're gonna have to tell your parents some version of the truth so they'll understand why it's important for them to stay here until I get back," I replied.

"Where you going?" Iree asked.

"I'm going to tie up all loose ends. I'ma make it understood that nobody fucks with what's mine."

# Chapter 10
## One week later
## Chicago

"May I help you?"

"How are you doing, Sister Trowell? Deacon Strong sent me down here with this fresh apple pie and asked me to give it to you," I said, smiling pleasantly.

"Oh, that was thoughtful of him, and of you for bringing it down here to me."

"It's no problem at all. Sister, I know firsthand the temperamental Chicago weather can make you want to stay indoors where it's safe," I replied.

"That is too true, young man. Why don't you come in and join me for a piece of that delicious pie you're holding, and I'll put on some coffee to knock the chill off of you," she offered.

"It would be my pleasure."

I handed her the pie, and she stepped back to let me inside her home. The doctor was like any woman of her generation with the plastic slip covers on the furniture, and pictures of white Jesus everywhere you turned to look. It was like stepping into the seventies and eighties, but I wasn't here to appraise the value of her home and its belongings. I was here to knock dominoes over.

"You've got a beautiful home, Sister Trowell, how long have you lived here?"

"My whole life, child. My daddy bought this house back when this was still referred to as the colored side of town, and I've never lived anywhere else," she said with pride, leading me to the kitchen.

"Do you need any help?"

"No, you're my guest so you just sit yourself at the table, and give me all the good church gossip," she replied.

"Well, how long has it been since you were there?" I asked.

"I tell you with my bad hip and my arthritis, it's hard to make the trip as regular as I'd like, but I was there for Christmas."

"Well, Mrs. Bradley had a healthy baby boy, and now Mrs. Fonsworth is pregnant," I said.

"Oooh, child! Trevor Fonsworth got fixed years ago!"

"But, Deacon Paulson didn't," I whispered, smiling.

Hearing this caused her to laugh until she had to stop what she was doing to catch her breath.

"I done heard it all now," she declared.

"You ain't even heard the half of it."

She quickly moved to the table with the pie, some plates, and forks, and sat down to give me her undivided attention. I brought her up to speed on all the whispers that I'd picked up on while attending last Sunday's service at the First United Baptist Church of Chicago, watching her eyes dance with delight. By the time the coffee was served, she knew who was fucking who, who came out of the closet, and who had their hand in the collection plate. For her, I was the bringer of rain, and we chatted like old friends until an hour of our lives had evaporated.

"Child, you definitely brightened my day, because I don't know when I've laughed so hard," she said.

"Laughter is good for the soul."

"Ain't that the truth. Do you want another cup of coffee?" she asked.

"Sure, I'll have another before I go."

I waited until she'd crossed to the stove before I got down to business.

"Is that your daughter?" I asked, pointing to one of the many pictures on the refrigerator.

"That's my grandbaby, Brianca, but I raised her like my own. Her mother was hooked on drugs and died of an overdose when she was two, so from that point on it was just me and her."

"I bet you two are close," I said, accepting the coffee cup she handed me.

"She's grown now and lives her own life, but she still calls me regularly. She's still my baby."

"Family is important, it's the ties that bind and all we can hold onto when the world shakes around us," I stated.

"Amen, child."

"Sister, Trowell, would you mind if I used your bathroom?"

"Not at all, baby, it's right down the hall, second door on your right," she replied, pointing behind her.

My smile remained on my face as I sat the cup down and stood up to move past her. I knew my sudden change of direction caught her by surprise, but by the time she figured out what was going on, her neck was broken and she'd gone limp in my arms. I carried her body into the living room and placed it at the bottom of the stairs, making it look like she'd fallen. It crossed my mind to break her hip for good measure, but the fun in that would've been doing it before I killed her. With the scene set, I went back into the kitchen and helped myself to another slice of pie while finishing my coffee. I made sure to wash my dishes and put the rest of the pie in the refrigerator before making my way back outside. As I was walking back down the street to my 2002 Buick Regal, I pulled my phone out and dialed a number.

"911 what's your emergency?"

"I just heard what sounded like a woman's scream as I was walking past a house," I said, sounding like a concerned citizen.

"What's the address, sir?"

I rattled off the late Mrs. Trowell's address and hung up. Once I was behind the wheel of my car and had driven several miles I tossed my phone out the window. I rode around the city waiting for it to get closer to darkness, before pointing my car in the direction of the First United Baptist Church of Chicago. A well-dressed black man carrying a shopping bag looked completely normal in this environment, and I strolled into the church with confidence. I moved swiftly through the building, stashing my presents until all that remained was the empty shopping bag. Forty-five minutes later, I was letting myself back into my hotel room and the Comfort Inn, where I came face-to-face with a serious looking Glock .17.

"Please don't shoot," I said, smiling.

"Only you shoot the people you love."

"Seriously, baby, you and my sister gotta let that go," I replied, closing and locking the door behind me.

"Oh, I've let it go, but I don't think she will until she gets some payback in the form of putting a bullet in you."

"If she's smart, she'll let go of those ambitions, and you shouldn't be encouraging her. What happens if she shoots me somewhere that affects my…performance?" I asked.

"Oh, hell nah, yeah…I'll definitely be talking to her when we get back," Honey replied seriously.

I laughed while crossing the room to give her a hug and kiss.

"Is everything okay? You seem jumpy," I said.

"Of course I'm jumpy, we're back in fucking Chicago not a month after you got shot!"

"It's okay, sweetheart, nobody knows we're here and we'll be gone in a few days," I replied soothingly.

"I just don't like being here, bae."

I could've reminded her that she forced me to bring her, but I'd wasted enough of my breath fighting her on that issue back in Mississippi. It still pissed me off that she'd brought up she'd saved my life the last time, because it was a blatant reminder of what not listening to her had almost cost me. Nobody liked hearing *I told you so*. She'd thought she was gonna talk her way into going with me to handle my business, but once she saw I was serious about smacking her over the head with my pistol, her tune had changed.

"Did you miss me?" I asked, trying to distract her.

"Is that a serious question?"

I kissed her again, making sure to convey with just my mouth how much I missed her. I felt her toss her gun aside as she found a better use for her hands in helping me out of my clothes. I waited until she had me down to nothing except my socks before I pulled off the t-shirt she'd been wearing.

"No underwear, I guess you did miss me," I said, rubbing her clit in slow clockwise circles.

"Uh-huh."

I gently pushed the tip of my finger inside her to gather some of her sweetness before bringing it to my mouth and sucking it off.

"Still good?" she asked.

"Is that a serious question?"

Our lips met again and our tongues fought to see who would get the last taste of her. She'd made it clear long ago that she loved the taste of her pussy as much as I did.

"I'm driving," she said huskily, spinning me around and pushing me down on the bed. With the patience and grace of a lioness stalking her prey, she climbed on top of me and slid down my dick with the controlled strength of a dancer. From the moment of complete penetration, her walls spoke of real love by holding me close enough to hurt. She hurt so good though. For a moment, she simply sat there with her hands on my chest and her eyes locked on mine. I loved the way we communicated in these moments like this because it combined the physical, mental and emotional without needing verbal interference. I knew she wouldn't move until she was ready, just like I knew taking her soft, succulent titties in my hands would only increase her hunger. This was the game we played, and we loved it. When I pinched her nipples, her eyes flashed brightly like hazard lights in the rain, making me smile. Using her arms for leverage, she raised herself slowly until only half of my dick was still in her, and then she quickly slammed down on me, fucking the air from my lungs. The smile of satisfaction on her face only made me pinch her nipples harder and fondle her titties rougher. And so the battle began. It was a long five minutes before she started riding me at a slow pace and in truth, we were both ready to cum, but we held on. When she took her hands off my chest I sat up, eager to let my lips and tongue replace my hands. Her rhythm never broke as I placed soft kisses all over both of her titties, before using my tongue to play tag with her hard nipples.

"Dameian," she moaned passionately.

When she moved her hips in slow circles, I bit her nipples to send the same pleasurable shocks through her body that she was giving me. Her increase in speed lit the fuse to our mutual hunger, making it clear we were on borrowed time. Suddenly, she pushed me flat on my back and I could tell by the look in her eyes that the animal I loved was loose.

"Beautiful s-savage," I mumbled.

"Only for-for you, baby."

This time when she put her hands on my chest, I put mine on her hips, and we moved in sync like a well-oiled piston. I bucked and she rode until the goal of mutual climax was reached with strangled screams and primal grunts. In the aftermath, I held her close and listened to her heartbeat communicate with mine, finally knowing what love sounded like.

"I can't lose you," I said.

"I'm glad you feel that way."

"I'm serious, Tabitha. I've lived my life with the firm belief that everyone I came into contact with was expendable, but I don't feel that way about you."

"You love me," she replied simply.

"It's more. It's more than love and being in love. It's...just *more*!"

When she raised her head to look at me I could see all that I felt mirrored in her eyes, even the things I wasn't saying.

"You're worried, aren't you?" she asked softly.

"I know the power of being the unseen hand of God, and I know how hard it is to fight what you can't see."

"But, are you worried though?" she persisted.

I thought about her question in terms of what the definition of that particular word was. I felt like if I ever worried, then I was doubting my skill set, and I was way too arrogant for that.

"No, I'm not worried," I replied simply

"Then, neither am I," she said, laying back on my chest.

"You know I'm not letting you go with me."

"I know," she replied softly, holding me tighter.

Bringing her with me to Chicago was one thing, but there was no way I'd take her anywhere near Florida. As soon as things were finished here, I was taking her back to Mississippi with her family and Iree.

"Did you call and check on everybody?" I asked.

"Yeah, my parents are keeping their eyes open, but everything has been quiet. Ray-Ray barely leaves your game room, my parents say that he's in there playing PlayStation five *all the time*. It keeps him busy. And Rain…well her and Iree get along really well."

"How well?" I asked hesitantly.

My wife's soft laughter said a lot more than her words.

"I can neither confirm nor deny your suspicions, but girls will be girls," she replied.

"Just keep your eyes on them when you get back."

My request made her silent, but I knew it was only because she didn't want to go back to Mississippi without me.

"How long will we be here?" she asked.

"It's typical to have a funeral within a week of someone dying."

"You sure Brianca will show up?" she asked.

"She'll be there."

"You sure Ghost is really dead?" she asked.

"As sure as I can be in the dental records Aubrey located for him."

"Dollar, I can't lose you."

"I'm glad you feel that way," I replied, smiling.

"Promise me you'll come back."

"I promise," I said, without hesitation.

"How long will you be gone?" she asked.

"You know I can't answer that."

"Well, how long will it take?" she persisted.

"As long as it takes, sweetheart."

I knew she wanted to hear guaranties, but I couldn't give those to her. I was flying completely blind into this situation. I couldn't put into words how frustrated I was at Aubrey's inability to find even the smallest clue as to who put a price tag on my wife's head, but that wouldn't deter me. My strategy was simple, I was going straight into the mud and getting as filthy as I could.

"Dollar?"

"Yes, baby?"

"Make love to me," she demanded.

"Yes, baby."

We made love long into the night until we finally fell asleep in each other's arms. The next two days was spent doing more of the same, but neither of us minded because what we had for each other was of the same intensity. By the third day though, it was time to get back to business because Ms. Norma Jean Trowell's viewing and funeral service were scheduled for the following day at First United Baptist church of Chicago. I waited until late into the night before going to reenter the church, and make sure that all the preparations I'd made were still ready. The service began at 11 am, and from my vantage point across the street, I saw that a lot of people loved Ms. Trowell. My interest was only in one mourner though and she showed up, looking classically sexy in her little black dress. Once Brianca entered, the doors to the church closed, and the sound of the organ signaled the beginning of the service. Still, I waited. Finally, after half an hour, I got into my car and prepared to leave. Before pulling off, I grabbed the device that appeared to be a normal keychain, and pressed the button in the center of it. Even though I was five blocks away, by the time Sister Trowell took to the sky to be with the Lord, I still felt the ground tremble. I tossed my now useless keychain out the window and drove straight back to the motel. When I got there, I didn't even have to get out of the car because Honey was already coming out, carrying our overnight bag.

"It's on the news already," she said, getting in the car.

"Oh yeah?"

"Yeah, you used enough C-4 to put a hole in the world," she replied.

"Well, I had to make sure it was done right," I said, smiling as I pulled off.

"What type of person blows up an entire building just to kill one person?"

"A determined one," I replied honestly.

"So, what's next?"

"You know what's next, bae," I said, looking at her.

"Yeah, I know. Just remember your promise."

# Chapter 11
## Two days later
## Florida

I heard the key slide into the lock and the door being pushed open, just before the hall light came on. I didn't move though. I heard the sound of a bag of some sort hit the floor and a long sigh of relief as a pair of heavy boots were kicked off of some tired feet. I still didn't move.

"Jackie?" he called out, moving in my direction slowly.

I looked to my left at the woman crying silently by the dim kitchen light, shaking my head to discourage her from responding in the slightest.

"Babe, are you here?" he called out, rounding the corner that had separated him from our seat at the kitchen table.

"Michael, if you reach for your gun, you're gonna be forced to watch someone you love die, and then you're gonna die," I said calmly.

I saw no fear in his eyes, only rapid calculation as he took in the whole scene in front of him, stopping on the silenced Glock .27 I was holding.

"You know me?" he asked.

"Sure, you're Micki blue eyes, or would you prefer that I call you Detective Michael Solo?"

"So, you know I'm a cop and you're still in my home pulling this shit? That ain't balls, that's pure stupidity," he said, shaking his head.

"Or maybe its sheer madness, Micki. Whatever it is I can promise you that it's not a joke, and I'm as real as the tattoo on your wife's right ass cheek."

I could tell by the way he flinched that he desperately wanted to make a move, and I hoped that he mistook the smile on my face as anything close to resembling weakness.

"Relax, Micki, I ain't fucked her or your daughter. Yet," I said, gesturing towards the two women sitting inches away from me.

"Just tell me what the fuck you want, so you can get out of here," he replied.

"What I want is simple really, I'm just here for some information. Tell me what you know about this woman," I said, holding up my phone with a recent picture of Honey on it.

"I have no idea who that is."

"Micki, you said that *too fast* to be telling the truth. Now, I know for a fact you're a crooked muthafucka, and that means you got a lot of information in that big ass head of yours. The question is, are you gonna give it up the easy way or the hard way?" I asked seriously.

"Like I said, I don't know who that bitch is."

"How old is your daughter, Michael?" I asked.

"She's seventeen, and you better not fucking think about it," he replied aggressively.

"Oh, I've thought about it several times in the last hour that we've all been sitting here getting to know each other," I confessed.

"Micki, just tell him whatever he wants to know," Jackie said, crying harder.

"I *don't* know her," he said through clenched teeth.

"Okay, Micki, let's say for a second that I believe you. Who do you know that would know her?" I asked.

"Depends on who she was running with."

"Last I heard, she was hanging around some dudes named Chris and Ronnie," I said.

"Well then, that bitch is probably as dead as they are," he replied smiling.

His smile irked me as much as his need to call my woman out of her name. A subtle cough from the barrel of my Glock erased his smile as quickly as it rendered his right hand useless.

"Bet that hurt, huh?" I asked.

"F-fuck you," he growled, cradling his bloody hand against his chest.

"If you keep being uncooperative, I'm gonna fuck your wife and your daughter in front of you. This is the last time I'm gonna ask you nicely. Who would know her?"

"T-Tori Hynel," he said.

"Now see, that wasn't so hard," I replied, smiling.

"You better fucking kill me, because I swear to God—"

He suddenly stopped talking and just stared at me with eyes full of hate.

"Don't let the fact that I just shot your wife in the face cause you to freeze up, finish your sentence. You swear to God, what?" I asked calmly.

It was easy to see that he had a lot to say, but self-preservation had a hold of him.

"Go ahead and say it, say what's on your mind with your bitch ass," I taunted, aiming the still smoking pistol at his daughter's head.

"I don't have anything to say," he mumbled.

"What about you, sweetheart, you got anything you wanna speak on?" I asked the still trembling girl who was covered in her mother's thoughts.

There was a look of shock in her eyes, but she still shook her head no.

"You've got some nice lips, I bet you can suck the skin off a dick, huh?" I asked curiously.

She didn't respond to what I'd said, but I could feel him tense up.

"Come here," I demanded.

Slowly, she rose from her seat and walked around the table until she was standing in front of me.

"Can you suck the skin off a dick?" I asked.

Immediately, she looked out the side of her eye at her father, but she knew he couldn't save her.

"Yes," she replied softly.

"I'm sorry, I didn't hear you. Can you answer like you're telling the truth, please?"

"Yes, I can suck dick, okay?"

"What does your young white ass know about sucking dick?" I asked, laughing.

"Pull your dick out and I'll show you," she challenged.

"Now, this is getting interesting. Tell me, Megan, can you suck dick with no hands?"

"Yeah," she replied confidently.

"Good because I'm not taking these zip ties off. Get on your knees," I said, standing up.

One look at Micki told me that everything in him wanted to rush me, but we both knew he wasn't faster than a speeding bullet. Megan dropped to her knees and opened her mouth wide.

"What are you waiting for, Micki?" I asked.

"Huh?" he replied, dumbfounded.

I moved around behind his daughter and put my gun to the back of her head.

"You can either put your dick in her mouth, or I can put a bullet in her brain, and then yours," I said calmly.

I could tell by the horror on his face he hoped I wasn't serious, but I knew the look in my eyes said loud and clear that hope didn't live here.

"That's-that's sick," he said.

"I know. You've got seventeen seconds to make your decision, or I'll make it for you," I replied, looking at my watch.

His eyes darted back and forth between my gun and his baby girl's face, the epitome of damned if I do, damned if I don't.

"Ten seconds," I said.

"Dad," Megan sobbed.

Still, he stood there frozen and helpless, despite all the power he thought he had when he walked into his house a short while ago.

"Five seconds," I said.

"Dad!" she shrieked frantically.

"Okay-o-okay," he said, fumbling with his zipper as he moved in front of her.

The shame in his blue eyes was clear to see, but that didn't stop him from pulling out his dick and shoving it in between her lips.

"Now let's see those skills you were bragging about," I said, nudging her in the back of the head with my gun.

There was hesitation in her movements, but she got to work. When Micki closed his eyes, I knew it wasn't pleasure that caused that reaction, it was self-hate.

"Look at her, Micki," I demanded.

When his eyes snapped open, they locked on mine and the rage in them was so palpable, I felt it graze my cheek with the heat of a bullet.

"Look at her," I repeated, jamming my gun into her head.

He complied, but when his dick got hard, his tears fell.

"You've got good technique, Megan, it's clear that you've done this before. I don't have all night though, so speed it up," I said.

The fact that she didn't need to be told twice made me wonder how close father and daughter really were.

"Do you know why I'm doing this, Micki? Because you're weak. You're just like so many other pussies' that hide behind that badge so they can act hard, but you're weak. Instead of dying like a man, you're getting a blow job from your own daughter! And you're enjoying it! You deserve to die," I said, raising my gun until it was winking at him.

When he opened his mouth to speak, two bullets pushed his tongue through the back of his head, sending him flying.

"You did a wonderful job, Megan, truly wonderful," I said.

"Pl-please don't kill me, I—"

I gave her the courtesy of not knowing the bullets were coming by shooting her in the back of the head. After tucking my gun, I calmly strolled out of the house and down the street to my car. Once I was secured in its confines, I began my search for any and all information on Tori Hynel, not surprised to discover she was a cop too. I took my time absorbing all the information that I could dig up on her, only committing to memory what would be useful to me now. I didn't like not having the time it took to do the research that Aubrey was famous for, but I was all too aware that given what was at stake time was a luxury I didn't have. Once I felt like I knew enough I started my car, and pointed it towards Tori's condo. A half an hour later, I was cruising past her building for the second time, studying the layout and the foot traffic. The area was nice, but according to Tori's latest tax return it was within her means, just like the 2015 Mustang she drove. Tori was smart because she didn't flaunt the fact that she was a dirty cop, and that she'd been at it for a while said she had no intention of changing her ways. This worked to my benefit because I know that meant she was up to date with the latest information. I hadn't spotted her car during either of my drive-bys, but she was a single, attractive white female, so she most likely enjoyed going out after work. I parked my car two blocks away and walked back to her building. The presence of a camera over the entrance to the building made the hat that I was wearing appropriate, and there was no hesitation in my movements as I punched in Tori's code to gain access to the building. Anyone who looked at the footage later would assume I was a close friend or family member to someone who lived here. Once I got to the door I needed, it took me fifteen seconds to pick the lock and let myself in. As expected, it was dark and quiet inside, but I still did a room to room search to be sure that I was alone for the moment. Given how meticulous Tori was about keeping the secrets of her life nice and tidy, I was surprised to find her condo a mess. She had clothes thrown everywhere, papers of all sorts covering a lot of different surfaces, and a kitchen littered with old takeout containers. I wasn't here to give her a discount on maid service though. I took a seat in the darkest corner of her bedroom with just my pistol and my determination to keep me company, and I waited. It was a full two hours before I heard her come through the front door, and much to my annoyance, she wasn't alone. Based on the sounds I was hearing though, I knew the thought of an intruder in her home would never cross her mind, until it was too late.

"Do-do you have a condom?" I heard her ask.

"No."

"Fuck it, I'm on the pill anyway," she said.

From there, the audible sounds of their lip boxing resumed and seconds later, two figures entered the room with one thing on their minds. The dude carrying Tori tossed her on the bed and they both started hurriedly pulling off their clothes. Within moments, they were naked and breathing hard with need. I was kind enough to wait until they were a good thirty seconds into fucking before I made my presence known.

"You can leave your dick in her, but if you move without my permission, you'll die with only the memory of what her pussy felt like. Understand?" I asked, pressing the barrel of the silencer to his temple.

"I'm s-sorry, I didn't know sh-she was married," he stammered.

"That's not my husband," Tori said fearfully.

"And she's not married," I clarified.

"Who-who are you?" Tori asked.

"The better question is what do I want, Detective," I replied.

I could tell by the look  her eyes the fact that I knew who she was registered differently with her then it had with Micki. He'd thought he could somehow intimidate me with that knowledge, but she understood how serious it was for me to have that knowledge and still be here.

"What do you want?" she asked.

"I wanna know what you know about this woman," I replied, holding up my phone so she could see Honey's picture.

"You picked now to have this conversation?" the man said.

"I can tell you're frustrated, and I apologize for the inconvenience."

I quickly pulled the trigger, and then pushed his lifeless body out of her and onto the floor. With him out of the way, I now had room to give her something hard and black.

"I know this is a little warm, but I'm sure that your pussy is hotter, so you'll be okay. I advise you not to make any sudden moves though because a bullet travelling through this part of your anatomy will definitely hurt." I warned.

"Please you-you don't have to d-do that. I know who you are. I'll talk," she replied, crying.

"What do you mean you know who I am?"

"If y-you're asking me about her, then you're the one I've heard stories about," she said.

"You've heard stories, huh? Entertain me with one," I requested.

"No one knows your name, but if the boogeyman and the devil built a monster, then that would be you. You were just here a few weeks ago. I saw-saw pictures of what was left of that b-baby."

"It wasn't my fault Chris used him as a shield. Enough about me though, tell me what you know about the woman in the picture," I said.

"I kn-know you're gonna kill me, but if I tell you what I know, will you promise not to make me suffer?"

I gave her request careful consideration while pushing my gun in and out of her pussy very slowly, staring deeply into her eyes.

"Let's see what you tell me first, Tori."

"T-Tabitha was supposed to have died in that house with everybody else, and when her body didn't turn up, it was assumed that she got away. So, a contract was put out for her."

"By who though, because I know it wasn't Pablo," I said.

"I don't know who exactly ordered the hit—"

"*Tori,*" I said, forcing my gun inside her harder.

"I swear! It came from someone in prison, that's all I know!" she insisted, crying harder.

I knew that someone making a call like that from behind the wall signified he definitely had power and friends.

"Which prison?"

"I don't know, I swear to God I don't know," she replied quickly.

"Calm down, Tori," I said, pulling the pistol all the way out of her.

I gave her a few moments to get herself under control while I thought of all the ways to attack this new piece of the puzzle.

"How do you know about the contracts?" I asked.

"I-I'm on the payroll for the Columbian Cartel, and they're somehow involved in whatever this is."

"How much do they pay you?" I asked.

"One hundred thousand a year."

"That's chump change to them, why are you settling for what equates to their lunch money?" I asked curiously.

"Because nobody negotiates with the Cartel."

"Ah, but you started off trying to negotiate with me, and you know what I'm about," I pointed out.

"I just d-don't wanna die slow," she said softly.

"Any more last requests?"

"It would've been decent of you to let us finish since you knew you were gonna kill us anyway," she replied.

Her response made me chuckle.

"I can always use my gun to finish you off," I offered.

"Thanks, but no thanks. Everything black and hard ain't pleasurable."

"Okay. If you answer my next question truthfully, I'll compromise with you," I said.

"What do you wanna know?"

"Who's running shit for the Columbians now?" I asked.

"That would be Juan Pedro, and he's ninety-five percent crazy," she replied.

"Good thing that I only believe in absolutes. Where are your handcuffs?"

"In my jeans on the floor," she said, nodding in the general direction.

"Get them and if you reach for your gun, I promise your death will be slow."

I got up off the bed with her and kept a close eye on every move she made. Once she passed me the cuffs, I secured her hands behind her back and led her to the bathroom.

"Step in the shower," I demanded, turning the hot water on.

When she was standing over the water's spray, I sat my gun down on the sink and took all of my clothes off.

"I won't rape you, but I will fuck you if you want me to," I offered.

"Please do," she replied, staring intently at my dick.

I stepped into the shower behind her, bent her over while taking a hold of her handcuffs, and pushed inside her. After a few strokes I could feel her body trembling, and within three minutes, she'd cum all over my dick. Before she was done shaking, I was washing my dick off and prepared to wash her pussy out.

"Wait, I-I wanna make a deal," she pleaded.

"I don't do deals."

"I know Juan Pedro's hangouts, and I know some females that he fucks regularly," she said quickly.

"I'll humor you, Tori, what do you want for this information? And don't ask me to spare your life because you know better," I stated.

"Just-just fuck me until sunrise."

This seemed like an odd request and a play for time, but when I looked in her eyes all I saw was hunger.

“Alright, but the cuffs stay on and we stay in the bathroom.”

Her response was to quickly turn around and bend back over. For the next three and a half hours we put all surfaces of her bathroom to use, and I fucked her like she’d never been fucked before. When we were done, I bathed her thoroughly, so that none of my DNA was on or in her body, and then I took her back into her bedroom. Once she’d told me everything she knew, I took her cuffs off, laid her flat on her back, stuck my gun underneath her left titty and pulled the trigger. Death was instant and she took it surprisingly, with a smile. After cleaning her bedroom, I left as quietly as I’d came, already mentally seeing my next victim.

# Chapter 12

"Hey, baby, did I wake you up?"

"Yeah, but it's okay. What's wrong?" I asked groggily, trying to see the time on my watch.

"Nothing. I saw that I missed your call this morning, but I got your message about you just getting in, so I decided to wait a while to call back."

"I'm glad you woke me up because I didn't mean to sleep until two pm," I said, sitting up in bed.

"Must've been a long night."

I could hear the questions she was asking all the way from Mississippi, but she was smart enough to know that no details would be discussed on the phone.

"Yeah, it was, but it was productive though," I replied.

"That's good, because I miss you. Do you know when you'll be home?"

"Not yet, bae, but how is everything there?" I asked, smoothly switching subjects.

"Everything is fine. My parents are enjoying their vacation, and I've been spending a lot of time with Ray-Ray."

"You haven't been spending time with Rain?" I asked concerned.

"She's been…busy," Honey replied vaguely.

"Tell me Iree didn't get to her."

"Bae, I don't know who got to who first, but when I stumbled upon them down by the creek, they were getting each other. *Thoroughly*!" she said, laughing.

"That damn sister of mine is a hot-ass mess! What did they say when you caught them?" I asked.

"Technically, they don't know I caught them, I mean, I didn't see the sense in making a big deal out of it. Plus, them bumping pussies means nobody is coming home pregnant."

"True shit. Do your parents suspect something?

"I ain't told them shit though, plus we're all pretty much content not to rock the boat of the unstable teenage female emotions," she replied seriously.

"God forbid that you do that."

"You joke because you ain't here to deal with the bullshit, and because you solve your problems using alternative methods," she said.

I laughed at her description for my willingness to shoot people behind the bullshit, even though it was true.

"Sorry, I got a low tolerance," I replied.

"Yeah, well I got a low tolerance for being without you, so you need to come home."

I should've known just because I'd changed the subject, that didn't mean she wouldn't change it back.

"Bae, you know that me being out here is necessary right now because if it wasn't, we'd be on some cheesy couples cruise, fucking up the headboard on a heart-shaped bed," I replied seriously.

"I'm telling you now, I'm gonna be soooo pissed at you if I don't get the honeymoon you promised, and I better get it soon too," she said aggressively.

"Yes, ma'am."

"I'm serious, Malcolm."

"I know you're serious, and I hear you loud and clear," I replied.

"Good. Don't make me fuck you up."

Her threat made me laugh, but only because I thought that she was being more serious then joking.

"I love you, I said.

"I love you more, but please don't make me kill you to prove that."

"I won't. Now if you're done threatening me I have a serious question to ask you," I said.

"Yes, my pussy is wet, it's wet every time I hear your voice, and I've been playing with it at least twice a day since you left. Next question please," she stated matter-of-factly.

"All of that is good to know, that's not where I was going. Who do you know in the prison system out here?"

Her immediate silence was a clear indicator that my assumption about her knowing somebody who was locked up was accurate. That was obviously good news and bad news.

"Wh-why do you think I know someone who's in prison out there?" she asked, hesitantly.

"One, because of your reaction right now and two, because of your reaction right now. Answer the question please."

For the first time since we'd known each other, I could feel her wanting to lie to me and that worried me. Not because of what she was hiding, but because she wanted to continue hiding it after she'd always been brutally honest.

"It's okay, sweetheart," I said soothingly.

"My-my baby's father is locked up down there, the one responsible for my oldest two."

"Okay. Did you and him end on bad terms?" I asked.

"According to him, we never *did* end, and we never *will* end. He's crazy."

Even without having all the pieces to the puzzle, this situation was starting to make a little more sense.

"When was the last time that you had any type of communication with him?" I asked.

"It's been more than a year, because it was before I started fucking with Chris. We haven't physically been together in years though."

"So, what's his problem?" I asked, trying to see what my best approach would be.

"He's crazy! He thinks he owns me and I'm supposed to do whatever the fuck he says, like I'm that same seventeen-year-old that he married. Well, I'm *not*!" she stated angrily.

"Whoa, whoa, hold up. Married? I don't believe we've ever had a conversation about you being married to this nigga."

"I didn't mention that?" she asked innocently.

"Don't be cute, Tabitha."

"But I thought that you liked when I was cute, Dameian."

I let my silence speak for me to avoid cussing her ass out because now was not the time to have our first fight. I listened patiently as she took a deep breath and searched for whatever words she intended to use.

"We were married for three years, he treated me like shit and beat on me, and I didn't escape until he got locked up. I made the mistake that a lot of young girls make by looking for a savior in the wrong type of dude," she said candidly.

I wanted to ask if she felt even the slightest bit of that now, given the current nigga she was married to, but this wasn't about us.

"Tell me what I need to know about him."

"I told you, *he's crazy*! The muthafucka is fifty years old and still gang bangin'!" she said disgustedly.

"Which gang?"

"Latin King, and—"

"King? This nigga must not be from out here," I said.

"No, he grew up in Chicago. He's got a lot of rank within his organization too."

Knowing that he was a King from Chicago put his brand of crazy into perspective. It also explained how Honey had been familiar enough on the dangers of the Vice Lords to follow me to my meeting with Brianca. Undoubtedly, she'd witnessed her ex go to war.

"Where is he?" I asked.

"The last I heard he was in the maximum security prison outside Tallahassee."

"And his name?" I asked.

"You know, I've answered every question you've asked me, and I think it's my turn to ask you something," she said.

"Okay, go ahead."

"Are you asking me this because you think he had something to do with your current job assignment?" she asked.

"I'm asking because every rock had to be looked under, and someone suggested I look behind the wall."

"I see," she replied shortly.

At this point I felt like she might actually be seeing clearer than I was able to right now, and that frustrated the shit out of me.

"His name?" I repeated.

"Joakeen."

"This nigga ain't a prince, so what's his last name?" I asked, becoming more frustrated by her bullshit.

"Alveraz."

"Aight, I need to look into some shit, but I'll call you later on," I said.

"You promise? I mean, I wouldn't ask, but you sound like you're pissed off at me," she replied.

"It wouldn't matter if I was pissed off at you, I still love you and of course I promise to call."

"I don't wanna fight with you, especially about bullshit from my past. All that matters to me is that you're my future," she said lovingly.

"Likewise. Now I'm gonna do what's necessary to make sure that future is long and bright. I love you, baby."

"I love you too, daddy," she purred.

The hair on the back of my neck stood up long after I'd hung up the phone, but my mind was back on business. I immediately sent Aubrey an encrypted email, telling her what information I needed, and then I took a nice long hot shower to clear away the last residuals of sleep. By the time I was finished bathing and dressed in some jeans and a t-shirt, Aubrey had sent me part of what I needed. Now that I had the ability to get to work right away, I packed up all my shit, tossed it in the back of my purple Chevy, and jumped on the highway. I used the miles ahead in front of me to contemplate exactly how I wanted to play this out. For some reason, I felt like the window of opportunity for me to fix this entire situation was closing rapidly, and that was only making my task more difficult. If whoever put the hit out on Honey decided to make it a contract open to every hitta, then the number of people who I had to kill was gonna grow. I never had a problem with adding more notches to my gun in the form of taking lives, but being distracted in a situation this serious would guarantee that I became somebody's notch. Within five hours, I reached Tallahassee and checked into a Red Roof Inn motel. As soon as I got in my room, I called Aubrey.

"It's me."

"I got the info you need, and the location of a safe house like you asked," she replied.

"Aight. I'm gonna hit the ground running, so I might be out of touch for a few days."

"You be safe," she said, hanging up.

I pulled my tablet from my bag and relaxed on the bed, while studying the next person in my crosshairs. After a couple hours I went out to grab something to eat, and then it was right back to plotting and planning with ruthless efficiency. Once I was comfortable and confident in a plan of action, I changed my clothes and got back on the move. Dressed in all black had me moving with the confidence of a shadow through the sleepy suburban neighborhood I'd arrived in, and within minutes I was at the house I wanted. The lights on in the living room allowed me to see the couple snuggled together on the couch in front of the TV, which meant now was the perfect time to sneak in through the open garage door. I quickly picked the lock on the door that separated the garage from the kitchen, and quietly stepped inside the house. The silenced Taurus 9mm appeared in my hand like magic and I let it lead the way into the living room.

"What are you watching?" I asked, stopping a few feet away from where they sat.

Both of them jumped and she quickly stifled her scream, sensing that continuing it would be a bad idea.

"Who-who are you? What are you doing in our home?" he asked, with more than a little aggression in his voice.

It always amazed me how men tended to take an aggressive stance or position in situations such as these, like somehow being macho wouldn't get their grapefruit busted. I was a man with a gun, not a dog barking that he could intimidate into backing off or sitting.

"Bravery is overrated," I said, shooting him twice in the chest.

"Please, please, please, please d-don't kill me, I'll do whatever you want, please," she begged, crying instantly and uncontrollably.

"What I want you to do is calm down so that you don't go into labor. You're eight months pregnant, right?"

"Yeah, pl-please don't hurt my baby," she said, trying to calm herself.

"Neither of you will be harmed as long as you do what I say. Understood?"

"Y-yes," she replied.

"Good, now I want you to put some shoes on because we're going for a little ride," I said.

Her movements were slow due to her size, but overall, pregnancy looked good on her. I'd seen pictures of her when she'd been barely one hundred and ten pounds, and wearing a size A-cup bra, but now she was every bit of one hundred and seventy pounds and them titties were borderline D-cups.

"Pregnancy suits you, Autumn, and after you have that baby, your body will snap back with some curves that will turn plenty of heads."

"You-you know my name?" she asked.

"Of course, you didn't think that I just ran up in random people's houses and asked them to go for a ride, did you?" I asked.

"Wh-what do you want with me?"

"Just to spend some time with you. Come on, let's go out through the garage," I insisted.

I made sure when we got outside, I kept my gun pressed against my side, so we would appear to be nothing more than two people out for a stroll. The fact that I'd ended her man's life without hesitation kept her from trying anything foolish, and I appreciated that. It took us five minutes to get to my car and another twenty-five minutes before we arrived at my secondary destination.

"Are you-are you gonna rape me?" she asked when I pulled up in the driveway of the safe house.

I turned to her and stared at her for a moment.

"Do you want me to rape you?"

"What type of sick question is that?" she asked.

"It's a proven fact that women of all ages, races, and cultural backgrounds have at some point in their life had a rape fantasy. I'm simply asking if you want me to fulfill yours."

Even in the darkness, I could see the blush creep up her face until her forehead was almost the shade of red as her hair color.

"Autumn, it's not my place to judge you, but it's probably best that you don't judge me either. Just because I'm a black man that kidnapped a white woman, doesn't mean that I'm gonna rape you, any more than it means that I'm gonna take you to the top of the tallest building in the city, where airplanes can gun me down," I said, smirking.

"I didn't mean-it's just, I'm pregnant. Even if I did have those fantasies before, I wouldn't want it to happen while I'm pregnant."

"Then it won't. Come on," I said, getting out of the car.

We made our way up to the front door where I knocked twice, and the door was immediately opened by a black dude wearing a mask.

"I'll call when I'm on my way back," I said, letting her move past me into the house.

I quickly got back behind the wheel of my car and headed back to Autumn's house. I put her dead fiancé in the trunk of the Volvo parked in the garage, and then I cleaned the crime scene to the best of my abilities. I didn't know who had access to her home or who would be stopping by, so I needed everything to look normal until my play was complete. By the time I was done with the clean-up it was 1:30 am, which meant I still had time to kill, so I turned off the lights and kicked back to watch TV. I waited until exactly 4 am before I picked up Autumn's cellphone off the coffee table and scrolled through her contacts until I found the number and name I was looking for. I made the call and he answered on the third ring.

"Sweetheart, what are you doing up this early in the morning? Is it time? Is the baby coming?"

"Mr. Plummer, this isn't your daughter. This is the man who had kidnapped you daughter," I stated calmly.

"The man who-who what? Put my Autumn on the phone."

"Wendell, I'm gonna need you to stop trying to make demands and listen to mine. That is, if you want to see your daughter and grandchild again," I said.

"I'm listening, I'm listening."

"Good. What I want is very simple, you have a prisoner under your supervision by the name of Joakeen Alveraz. He needs to meet with an unfortunate accident that he can never recover from, do you understand?" I asked.

"I-I understand."

"Excellent, Warden Plummer, that's just excellent. I think I'm offering you more than an even trade, Warden, but if you try to play me in any way, I'll take more from you than I already have. I'll kill Autumn, your wife Martha, her sister Cindy, your brother Bobby, and your dog Spot. You've got seventy-two hours, Warden," I said, hanging up.

I made sure to leave Autumn's phone at the bottom of a bowl of bleach before I left her house and headed back to my car. I was feeling the fatigue and glad to be headed back to my motel room, so I wasted no time getting on the road. It wasn't until I had almost reached the dream of my bed that I realized I had missed calls from both Iree and Honey. Naturally, I called Honey first, but after not getting a response to three separate attempts, I assumed she was asleep and called my sister instead.

"Dollar?"

"You sound wide awake at almost five am, that can only mean you're up to no good," I said.

"No, I'm not. Dollar you need to come home *now*!"

"Wh-what's wrong?" I asked quickly.

"It's Honey. She's gone."

# Chapter 13

"What the fuck do you mean, Honey's gone?"

"I mean she got in the car and left," Iree said.

"Oh. She probably went for drive or to the store—"

"No, Dollar she packed a bag and told her parents not to leave under any circumstances," Iree explained.

The surge of anger I felt translated into my feet being heavy on the gas and my car rapidly picking up speed, but I knew I had to keep my voice calm.

"Did she give you any type of indication where she was going?" I asked.

"No, and I begged her not to leave until she talked to you, but she said you were busy."

To my ears that sounded like Honey was on some do-it-yourself shit, which was a recipe for disaster.

"Aight, I'll deal with it, you just make sure you stay at the house," I said.

"There's something else that you should know. Before she left, she gave me a gun."

"Do you know how to shoot?" I asked.

"You raised me, didn't you?" she replied.

"That's my girl. If you see anything out of the ordinary, I want you to shoot first and ask questions last, okay?"

"Understood. I love you, Dad."

"I love you too, Daughter," I replied, hanging up as I pulled into the motel parking lot.

I was already calling Honey's phone again before I made it inside my room, and my frustration was growing with every unanswered ring. I tried calling her two more times before finally sending her a text message, telling her to get her muthafuckin' ass back to the house before I got mad.

Truthfully, I was beyond mad already because I was supposed to be completely focused on the task at hand, instead of running behind her hard-headed, renegade ass! It was shit like this that made a muthafucka catch a domestic violence case for real. After another half-hour of trying in vain to get her to answer my calls and texts, I said fuck it and made a different call.

"It's me," I said.

"It's early."

"Yeah, I know, but my wife has gone rogue and I need you to find her," I replied.

"Damn, bruh, is the honeymoon over that quick?"

"Not now, Aubrey."

"Okay, okay. Well, at least I finally get to know her name since your ass has been tight-lipped," she said.

"You already know her name. It used to be Tabitha Dewhit."

"I'm sorry, did you say what I think you just said?" she asked slowly.

"You heard me, Aubrey."

"I'm gonna assume you're being serious because that puts your reaction to the job request into perspective, but why the fuck didn't you tell me sooner, Dollar? You don't trust me now?"

I could hear the hurt in her voice, and I'd always known it would be there, which was why I'd been dragging my feet about having this conversation. Aubrey was family and I loved her, but I trusted no one. That was hazardous to my health.

"You know it's not about that," I replied, deflecting the question.

"If it's not about trust, then what's it about?"

"My sole focus from the moment that you sent that email had been protecting her at all costs, and everything outside of that has been background noise. I apologize that your feelings were included in that, but you know me, sis, so you know how out of character this whole relationship is. I love her though, and that's why I'm all about one thing right now," I said truthfully.

I knew what I'd said probably wouldn't make Aubrey feel any better about being somewhat outside of my immediate circle right now, but she knew I was being real with her.

"I want you to be happy, Dollar, and you know that, but secrets between you and I can only hurt us in the long run. Don't do that, because you already know I love you too much to do it."

"I won't," I replied.

"Aight. Now since you woke me up, I guess I gotta get to work on this for you. What you gotta do is get some sleep, because being unfocused equals one thing and one thing only."

"Enough said. Thanks, sis," I replied, hanging up.

As badly as I wanted to say fuck sleep in favor of hitting the streets to find Honey, the reality was that I didn't know where to look, and Aubrey was right. So, with my gun in one hand and my phone in the other, I laid on the bed and closed my eyes. It took the usage of meditation techniques that I'd learned to block out all the noise in my head and coax sleep out of its hiding place, but I managed to do it. The feeling of my phone vibrating in my hand snatched me back though, and I answered it without opening my eyes.

"Yeah?"

"I was able to track your girl's phone, and you're not gonna believe where she's at right now," Aubrey said.

"Where?"

"A certain maximum security prison not far from you," she replied.

"*Mutha-fucka*!" I growled angrily, sitting up and swinging my feet to the floor.

"I'm gonna take your response to mean that all this shit is connected, but I'm not gonna get mad right now about how much I don't know. Just tell me what's next."

"I'll call you back," I said, hanging up.

I immediately dialed Honey's number, but this time I wasn't surprised when she didn't answer. After making sure I had my keys, I tucked my gun in my jeans, put my phone in my pocket, and I was out the door. I knew that speeding through a city I didn't know, with a gun on me that had a fresh body attached to it was a reckless move, but I didn't give a fuck. Fifteen minutes later, I eased into the parking lot of the prison and backed in, right next to a Black Lincoln with Mississippi plates. I'd only been sitting there a couple minutes, trying to figure out what my next move was, when I caught sight of Honey headed in my direction. It was evident she was distracted, or she would've noticed my car long before she walked up on it. By the time she did notice it though, I was standing with the driver's side door open, trying to stare a hole through her goddamn head.

"Oh shit," she mumbled.

A big part of me was contemplating shooting out both of her knees and throwing her in my trunk, but I knew that would definitely cause a scene.

"Follow me," I demanded, sliding back behind the wheel of my car.

Once she was in the driver's seat of the Lincoln, I started my car and pulled off. Doing the actual speed limit took us half an hour to make it back to my motel room, and during the entire ride I still couldn't figure out how I wanted to handle this. I was trying to let my rational mind take over, but the rage in me just kept building and building. By the time we were in my room with the door closed, the rage had blinded me.

"Baby, I—"

That was all she got to say before my left hand wrapped around her throat and my right hand pressed my gun to her forehead. I didn't say anything because I couldn't, but the fear in her eyes told me she could see everything I was feeling in my eyes.

"Dollar," she croaked.

My grip on her throat tightened as I cocked the hammer on my pistol. I could tell by the redness of her face that I was cutting off her air supply, but that was okay because the whisper from the monster inside me was telling me to pull the trigger. That would definitely solve the problem of her needing oxygen at all. When she raised her hand, I thought she was gonna try to pry my fingers from around her throat, but instead she wiped the tear from my cheek I didn't know was there. Somehow, what she did allowed me to slam the door on the unspeakable things that were driving me at this moment, and I lowered my gun. When I let it drop to the floor, I grabbed her face in my hands and kissed her with more passion and love than I ever had anyone in my entire life. Suddenly, our hands were moving as fast as our tongues were, and we were literally ripping each other's clothes off. She still had one leg in her jeans and my jeans were tangled around my ankles when I picked her up, pinned her to the wall, and shoved my dick inside her tight pussy. She didn't have to tell me to fuck her, and she didn't have to tell me how hard she wanted it, because I was trying to put her through the wall with every stroke. She was wetter than I'd ever felt her, so it didn't surprise me when she came with the beauty and suddenness of a summer rain cloud, but I fucked her right through it and into the next storm.

"Ah! Ah-oh God!" she screamed, clutching me tighter as wave number-two rolled her in its current.

I could feel her squirting all over me and her cum running down my legs, but that only made me pound her harder. Passion and purpose was the only way to deserve how my dick was banging at her pussy walls, testing their strength and durability while bathing in her pocket of rain.

"Oh-oh fuck, fuck, *fuck*!" she moaned, announcing the arrival of the sweetest death ever.

When her orgasm snatched the breath from her soul, I breathed life into her by cumming so hard that my knees wobbled unsteadily, but still I didn't stop moving inside her until her body ceased trembling. I let her down off the wall and took a seat on the bed, avoiding making eye contact with her as I tried to organize my chaotic feelings.

"Do I even wanna know what that was that just happened between us?" she asked, her voice scratchy and hoarse.

"It was sex."

"Don't lie to me, Dameian."

"Don't call me Dameian," I said, looking at her.

"So, I've lost the right to use your name now? Why didn't you just shoot me?"

"Don't tempt me," I replied seriously.

Her response was to pick up my gun and walk over to me.

"Here you go, but make sure you aim right here," she said, unhooking her bra and lifting her left tittie.

I took the gun and put it right where she'd requested, staring at her beautiful face intently.

"What are you waiting for?" she asked, when I hesitated.

I didn't think she truly understood how close I was to doing it, but what disturbed me more was that I didn't think she cared.

"Why do you want me to kill you all of a sudden?" I asked.

"Why have you stopped loving me all of a sudden?"

"I never said I didn't love you," I replied.

"No, but your actions damn sure are. We just shared a moment of epic proportions, and now you're treating me like you just fucked a beautiful stranger."

"Well, you are beautiful, and it's becoming increasing clear that I don't know who the fuck you are," I said seriously.

"I'm the bitch that's had to do for herself and take care of herself because no man has ever been able to, so that means I'm not good at letting people handle situations for me."

"Is that supposed to make me feel better about you going to have a face-to-face with the muthafucka who's trying to kill you?" I asked, sarcastically.

"Feel better? No. Understand why? Yes. I didn't do it to hurt you or your ego."

"This ain't about my goddamn ego," I growled, squeezing the trigger slightly.

"Then what's it about?" she asked.

"It's about you risking your fucking life when I'm out here doing all that, I can to *save you!* It's about you not knowing how to keep your goddamn word! It's about us!" I yelled, hating the fact that my voice was cracking.

"What about us?" she asked softly.

"I told you, I can't lose you. I'll lose what's left of myself."

"I'm gonna need you to explain that," she replied, taking the gun from my hand, and sitting beside me on the bed.

"Tabitha, you know who I am and what I am, and that doesn't allow me to feel anything. But, when I'm with you, I-I *feel*. When I'm with you, death is not everywhere around me. Don't get me wrong, because I love killing, but it's nice to love something more than that for once. Only one other person has made me feel anything close to what exists between you and I, and that ended badly."

"Baby, we won't end badly, I promise. If that means that I have to do what you say and let you take care of me, then I guess I'll struggle through," she said, smiling.

Despite still being angry with her, I smiled too as I pulled her towards me and kissed her.

"Just to be clear though, if you ever pull some shit like this again, I will shoot you," I promised.

"Really?"

"I-I sure-uh—"

The fact that she pushed me back on the bed and took my dick in her mouth affected my speech, and my train of thought, but she was making it hard to stay mad at her. Watching my dick disappear between her lips and down her throat was the world's best magic trick, but I couldn't let her have all the fun.

"Six-sixty-nine," I panted, pulling her towards me.

She stopped long enough to swing that good pussy in my direction, and then we both got to eat our favorite meal. A pleasurable twenty minutes passed before we finally surrendered to each other and laid down, side by side.

"If this is what h-happens when we fight, I'm gonna start picking fights," she vowed.

"Don't even think about it."

"This is mine, and I'll do what I damn well please to get it," she said, grabbing ahold of my dick.

“You keep being hard-headed and your ass is going on dick restriction.”

“Only my ass? Not my mouth and pussy?” she asked sarcastically.

“I mean it, Tabitha. I don’t handle fear well, and you…”

“I scared you and I’m sorry,” she said sincerely.

We laid in silence for a while until she flipped around so she could lay her head on my chest.

“So, what did your baby daddy have to say?” I asked curiously.

“I didn’t get to talk to him. He got stabbed to death on the way to breakfast.”

“How do you feel about that?” I asked.

“Relieved. I was tired of looking over my shoulder,” she replied honestly.

“I still don’t understand why you risked your life and came all the way down here.”

“Just the thought of that muthafucka still tormenting me, after all the years I put up with his bullshit pushed me into that ‘I don’t give a fuck’ mentality, and I wanted to tell him that face-to-face. I wanted to look him in his eyes and let him know that no matter what happened, he wouldn’t win because I wouldn’t cower like some small child,” she replied.

“You didn’t think I would’ve understood that if you had taken the time to explain it to me?” I asked.

“Oh, I knew you’d understand, but you still would’ve told me to stay my ass in Mississippi, so this was a situation where I had to ask for forgiveness instead of permission.”

“I’m not the forgiving type,” I reminded her.

“For the woman you love, you are. Besides, I was never really in danger anyway because I knew you were out here somewhere.”

"That type of logic will get you fucked up, sweetheart," I warned.

"You mean it'll get me fucked up against a wall," she countered giggling.

I gave her a love tap upside the head for her attempt at humor.

"I love you, Dameian."

"I love you, Tabitha."

"Don't call me that," she said, hitting me.

"I love you my sweet, sweet, Honey."

"That's better. Can we go home now?" she asked.

"I've still got some loose ends to tie up, the first of which is dealing with the warden's pregnant daughter," I replied, reluctantly sitting up.

"How pregnant is she?"

"Eight months, why?" I asked, looking at her.

"Let her live."

"Bae, you know that ain't how the game goes, especially since she's seen my face," I said.

"I'm pretty sure before you did anything else, you made sure her and her father knew how bad it would be to fuck with you. Let her live."

The fact that I was even debating on what course of action to take spoke to how much my wife meant to me. She wasn't just asking me to spare two lives, she was asking me to risk my life simply because she asked me to. It wasn't about the logic of a situation or even weighing out the odds, it was about her feeling like there was nothing in the world that I wouldn't do for her. I reached down into the pocket of the jeans still wrapped around my ankles, pulled out my phone, and made the call.

"It's me. Blindfold her, take her somewhere and let her go," I said, hanging up.

"Is there anything else that I can do for you, my queen?" I asked.

"Love me."

"Don't state the obvious, baby, because I'm always gonna love you," I said seriously.

"Okay. Well, you could put all of your loose ends on hold, and keep your promise to me."

"And which promise is that?" I asked.

"I believe you did promise me a honeymoon, a cruise to be exact."

"You're right, I did. You wanna go now though?" I asked.

"I do. Let's run away together."

# Chapter 14
## Miami
## Ten days later

"I cannot believe how much fun that actually was!" she said, taking my hand as we left the ship.

"I can't lie, I expected it to be really corny, but it was cool. Even though we didn't leave our cabin for the first two days."

"Nah, you're not about to blame me for that, when it was you who was in awe with the mirror on the ceiling," she said, elbowing me.

"You can blame me all you want to, but the way your ass jiggled as you popped your pussy on my dick was a thing of gorgeous booty-I mean beauty," I replied, pulling her into my arms once we reached our cars in the parking lot.

I'd travelled all around the world, but I'd never taken a vacation or taken the time to appreciate the things around me. Before this cruise, I hadn't realized how much of a workaholic I was, but the amazing woman in my arms was opening my eyes to all that I hadn't see. She was making it hard for things to ever be the same again, but I was more than okay with that.

"I'm glad that you appreciate my booty and my beauty, and I hope that you know how much I appreciate all of you?" she asked seductively.

"Absolutely."

That naughty twinkle was in her eyes, and I loved it. I loved that she was down for whatever whenever just like I was.

"As tempted as I am, I'm going to take my raincheck because we need to get home before my parents kill those kids," she said, smiling.

"When I spoke to your mom, she said that everything was fine, bae."

"That was probably before she walked in on Iree eating Rain like an ice cream sundae on a hot August day. And that's Mom's description, not mine," she said.

"Oh damn," I replied, already imagining the mortified look on her mom's face after witnessing that.

"Exactly, so let's get on the road, and I want to drive the Chevy."

"Why you wanna drive my Chevy all of a sudden?" I asked with mock irritation.

"Oh, it's not sudden, I been wanting to drive it since that first day. You know purple is my favorite color."

"You may have mentioned that," I said, pulling the keys from my pocket.

She passed me the keys to the Lincoln, gave me a quick kiss, and hopped behind the wheel.

"Don't drive fast," I said, motioning that there was a gun under the driver's seat.

She did the same gesture and when I got behind the wheel of the Lincoln, I reached under the seat and grabbed a Glock .45. Sitting it in my lap, I started the car and followed out of the parking lot. It was a comical sight to see her little ass trying to peep over the hood of my Chevy, especially with the car being raised in the front and dropped in the back. If she managed to handle it though, I was gonna give it to her. I'd give her anything to see that beautiful smile light up her face. I could tell she was still trying to get a feel for the car, because when the light we were coming to turned yellow, she hit the brakes instead of gunning it and floating through it. This made me chuckle, but the smile quickly evaporated from my face when a gray van slid to a stop next to her, the side door opened, and an AK-17 came out. For me, everything happened in slow motion but in real time, it all only took a few seconds to turn a beautiful day into something ugly. By the time the first round leapt from the barrel of the chopper, I had my pistol in my hand and I was dumping bullets through my windshield at the van. It was this and Honey's quick reaction, that turned the disadvantage of being caught by surprise into a level playing field. As soon as the shooting started, Honey pulled off, zigzagging through the blaring horns of opposing traffic. The van gave chase, but so did I and when I pulled up alongside them, I let my gun explain why this was a bad idea for them. The van quickly swerved in the opposite direction, allowing us to make a run for it, but I knew that wasn't gonna work. When I looked out of what was left of my windshield, I saw that my Chevy had come to a stop up against a parked car, with no movement inside. I pulled up beside it, hitting the ground at a dead sprint to get to her. When I snatched the door open, I had to beat back the panic trying to rip from my chest at the sight of her bleeding and slumped over on the seat.

"It's okay, baby, I got you," I said, scooping her up into my arms openly.

"Ahhh!" she shrieked in pain.

I didn't want to hurt her, but the relief I felt at hearing that she was alive had me running back to my car. Once I laid her across the backseat, I jumped back behind the wheel, and left a trail of smoke and rubber behind us.

"Talk to me, bae, how many times did you get hit?"

"I-I don't-don't know," she growled in pain.

"Where does it hurt?"

"My-my side, and my l-leg," she panted.

"Okay, just hold on while I get you to the hospital."

"You can't t-take me to th-the—"

"I most certainly can and since I'm driving, there's no way for you to stop me," I said.

"The p-police, bae—"

"Fuck the police!" I stated passionately, swerving in and out of traffic better than anyone in NASCAR history.

I knew she was worried because hospitals had to report all gunshot wounds, and cops had to ask all types of questions. Questions I could handle, but her dying…that wasn't even something I was prepared to think about. It was the longest ten minutes of my life before I pulled up in front of Miami-Dade Hospital, but the sound of Honey still moaning in the backseat let me know she was still alive.

"Help!" I yelled, as soon as I hopped out of the car, and tucked my pistol at the small of my back.

By the time I pulled her from the backseat, there were three nurses rushing my way with a stretcher.

"What do we got?" a tall brunette asked.

"She was shot, at least twice," I replied.

"How long ago?"

"About ten minutes," I said.

"Can you tell me your name, sweetie?" a short blonde asked.

"T-Tabitha Joyner," she replied weakly.

"Okay, Tabitha, we're gonna take care of you, alright? Just hang in there," the brunette said.

They took off with her on the stretcher at a high rate of speed, and me hot on their ass. I couldn't understand all the medical jargon they were using, but I'd shot enough muthafuckas to know that Honey was losing blood too fast for this situation to end the way I wanted.

"Sir, you have to wait here, we got her now," the blonde nurse said, holding me up outside the door to surgery.

"I love you, Honey!" I hollered.

"I l-love you too."

When she disappeared behind those doors, she took my heart with her, and all I could do was hope that she came back to me. As hard as it was, I knew I had to detach myself emotionally so I could solve this mystery surrounding what the fuck had just happened. I wanted to stay here and be here when she came out of surgery, but I needed answers. More importantly, I needed to kill a muthafucka. I got my phone out of my pocket once I made it back to my car, and was dialing while pulling off.

"It's me."

"Welcome back. Did you have a nice—"

"Aubrey, I need you to listen to me very closely and very carefully. We got off the boat, got in the car and two blocks later, a drive-by happened. I don't know the street we were on, but we were heading west. I need you to pull that traffic cam footage, copy it, erase it, then study it," I demanded.

"Are you hit?"

"No, but Honey is and it's bad," I replied softly.

"I'm so sorry, bruh, but I'm on it. Is there anything else you need?"

"Guns and a safe house," I replied.

"I'm on it, I'll call you back," she said, hanging up.

With that out of the way, I retraced the route I'd taken, not surprised to see the cops on scene already. I didn't stop or slow down, but instead turned my car in the direction the van had fled. I was now entering a residential neighborhood, which allowed me to cruise slowly without attracting suspicion from the locals. My eyes scanned both sides of the street with the intensity and skill of a seasoned hunter, thirsting for the prey I sought. I was three streets up when I caught sight of the crowd growing around a minivan that had lost a fight with a fire hydrant. I whipped my car up the side street, stopping just short of the crowd, and hopped out. I approached the group of five people with the same curiosity as the rest of the people rubber necking.

"Is anybody hurt?" I asked with fake concern.

"The two in here look dead, but one took off down the street a few moments ago," an older white lady said, pointing further up the street we were on.

Everyone was so consumed with the sight of dead bodies and bullet holes, that my retreat went unnoticed. Within seconds, I was back behind the wheel, hunting. I wanted to speed off, but I knew that would almost certainly be remembered by somebody, so I resisted the urge. At the end of the street was a four-way stop sign. Nobody was out and about, but I could see a lone figure to my right jogging away from me. I kept my speed at a normal cruise level, which brought me alongside the man within seconds. I took a glance around before raising my gun and firing out my passenger side window. My shot to the leg put him on the ground instantly, allowing me time to put my car in park, pop the trunk, and hop out.

"Let me help you," I said, smacking him viciously over the head with my pistol.

I quickly lifted his unconscious body and stashed him in the trunk, before climbing back behind the wheel and pulling off like nothing happened. My impatience had me wanting to search for a motel room to torture this nigga in, but I knew that wasn't the move a smart person would make, so I drove around aimlessly. I was just about to call Aubrey back after fifteen minutes of pointless driving, when she texted me a secure location. It only took me twenty minutes to get to the house that sat quietly at the end of a dirt road. As soon as I pulled up, the front door opened and a tall, petite black girl stepped out on the porch cradling an AK-47 in her arms.

"Name?" she asked, when I got out of the car.

"Dollar."

"What do you need first?" she asked.

"A place to kill somebody," I replied.

"Take him around back."

Once I grabbed dude out of the trunk I threw him over my shoulder, and carried him to the back of the house. The girl pointed towards a huge cypress tree about ten feet away and when I got to it, I saw that there were chains and shackles drilled into the trunk. After relieving my man of all his clothing, I strung his ass up.

"Use this," she said, handing me a thick bullwhip.

I wasted no time swinging that muthafucka with all my might and carving a nice piece of flesh from his back, bringing him back to consciousness with screams of pain.

"Screaming won't help and it won't save you. Nothing will save you because you're gonna die, but how much pain you endure first depends on you. Now, who sent you?" I asked.

Despite his obvious pain, his eyes blazed with defiance. I knew mine blazed in hunger. I cracked the whip again, this time taking blood and meat from his chest as he screamed and struggled uselessly against his restraints.

"Who sent you?" I asked again.

"He won't talk," the girl stated confidently.

I turned to face her and waited for an explanation.

"He's Columbian. If he talks, then they kill whatever family he has here, and whoever means anything to him in Columbia," she said.

Just knowing that he was Columbian meant he didn't have to talk, because I knew who'd sent him.

"You got any gasoline around here?" I asked.

"I'll be right back."

While she went to get it for me, I turned back to my Columbian friend hanging from the tree.

"I'm gonna beat you now. I'm gonna beat the skin off of you like I'm an angry slave master, and then I'm gonna burn you alive, so I can inhale the aroma of your flesh cooking. If you know anything about me, then you know that I'm a man of my word," I said calmly.

The defiance was still in his eyes, but so was the fear. The fear fed my hunger. Without delay, I began to make good on my promise, swinging the whip again and again. When the fatigue set in, I switched arms and when that arm started to hurt, I ignored the pain while thinking about the woman I loved, fighting for her life somewhere. Even when he went unconscious because of the pain, I continued whipping him. When I finally stopped my clothes were drenched with sweat, I could barely raise my arms, and the man in front of me looked like nothing more than rotted meat.

"You didn't ask him another question," she said, from behind me.

"I didn't need to," I replied, holding my hand out for the gas can.

Once she passed me that and the lighter, I doused him until the can was empty, and then I unhooked him from the shackles, letting his body hit the ground.

"Ashes to ashes, dust to dirt," I said, tossing the flame on him.

His screams were a thing of beauty and watching him flail around was like seeing bacon cook. I stood there and enjoyed the whole show, taking deep breaths until the smell of him was permanently imbedded on my brain and stuck in my throat. When there was no more to see, I pulled my gun out and aimed it with the intentions of filling his body full of more hot shit.

"You should save your bullets for someone who can feel them," she said.

"I need a shower."

"Follow me," she said.

She led the way into the house and gave me everything I needed to get clean, including a sweat suit to put on. I took my time under the water's spray, plotting my next move, step by step, body by body. It had been my intention to take my wife back to Mississippi and care for her the same way she'd done for me, but first I had some things that needed doing out here. After I was done showering and gotten dressed, I called Aubrey back.

"Tell me something," I said.

"Based on my tracking of your movements, I'm pretty sure you know as much as I do when it comes to the shooters, which probably means you know who sent them. What you don't know is that they weren't just after her, they were after you too."

"You're telling me that this muthafucka' Juan Pedro is crazy enough to come after *me*?" I asked.

"I'm not sure it's just him and his people, because I got a message saying the party who hired you for your wife is unhappy that they haven't seen results."

"When did you get this message?" I asked, confused.

"A little while ago when I started putting out feelers to find out what the business was."

"But that's not possible, because the second party has already been eliminated from the equation," I said, getting a bad feeling.

"Are you sure about that?" she asked.

I actually wasn't sure because I never had any type of communication with Joakeen before he died. I'd put the pieces of the puzzle together to fit the picture in my mind, but what if I'd made a miscalculation? No, that wasn't the right way to describe my wife being on somebody's operating table. What if I'd fucked up?

"Aubrey, you gotta be able to find out who'd behind this shit, because I'm fighting with one eye open out here."

"I'm doing my best, Dollar, but we both know there's one muthafucka who absolutely knows what's going on," she replied.

"Yeah, and I know how to get to him."

"Dollar, you know I never tell you how to handle your business, but I know this ain't business for you, which means you're entirely too close to see clearly. I'm asking you as someone who loves you and knows you, please take the necessary time to regroup."

The darkness that drove me couldn't even consider doing what she was saying, but the light that was my Honey was able to acknowledge I was moving purely off of emotion right now. The stakes were too high to play the game that way.

"Hear you, but I can't take her back to her family shot up," I replied.

"So, where do you wanna go?"

"They're expecting us to run, right? So, we do the opposite. We hide in plain view."

# Chapter 15
## Four days later

"Has the nurse said anything to you about being in the bed with me? You know they frown on that," she said weakly.

"I handled it," I replied, feeling relief in a way that was unspeakable at hearing her voice.

"You didn't kill her, did you?"

"No comment," I said, chuckling softly.

"Baby, everything hurts, how many times did I get shot?"

"You got hit three times and it took thirty years off my life, because I had to bargain with God to save you," I said.

"You talked to God?"

"Don't sound so surprised, I've prayed before. I just don't pray for myself, because that would be pointless," I replied.

"I prayed for you when you got shot, so it would seem that God hears us heathen-ass sinners. How long have I been unconscious?" she asked, trying to clear her throat.

I grabbed a bottle of water off the table next to me, put a straw in it and guided it to her lips.

"Drink this," I said.

She quickly followed instructions, still not opening her eyes, but back with me just the same.

"Th-thank you, bae. It felt like I had sweaters stuck in my throat."

It felt good to laugh after days of being on pins and needles with worry and fear. I'd thought she'd scared me when she'd made the trip to Florida unannounced, but her almost dying had taken shit to another level for real.

"I'll be honest, it crossed my mind to try and slide some of my cum down your throat in hopes that it would be the secret elixir to wake you up, but I know how much you love drinking straight from the tap," I said.

"I don't know what ghetto ass fairytale you grew up with, but Sleeping Beauty was awakened with a kiss, not a sample of really good semen."

"Tomato, tomato. You get my point," I replied, laughing.

"Yeah, that your arrogant ass thinks your cum will give a bitch life."

Her statement caused the laughter to die in my throat as sadness replaced it.

"What's wrong?" she asked.

"There's so much, where do I even begin?"

"How long was I unconscious?" she asked again.

"Four days."

"That means it must've really been bad," she commented.

"You were shot twice in the side and once in the left leg, and chopper bullets don't play nice," I said.

"Yeah, but you should see the other guy."

"You're not funny," I said, smiling.

"My eyes might be closed, but I can hear you smiling. Plus, I know I'm funny as fuck," she replied, smiling too.

It was great to see her smile, but given what I had to tell her, I didn't know how much of that she'd be doing. I was still trying to process my own grief, but mine would take a backseat to hers, once I found the words I needed to explain our loss to her.

"Unless you've dozed off, your silence is very loud. Whatever it is you're struggling to tell me is not gonna be made better by pretty words, so just tell me," she said.

"You were pregnant."

Now, it was her silence that was loud but I understood it, because I shared her pain.

"You said were…which means I'm not pregnant anymore."

"No," I whispered.

"Well, that sucks."

Her expression may have been one of lightheartedness, but the tears leaking from her closed eyes spoke of devastation. I wrapped my arms around her the best I could and held her while she cried silently. The most common thing for people to do in situations like this was assign blame to someone or something for this tragedy, but I knew right now, we were sharing the blame.

"How-how far along was I?" she asked emotionally.

"A little more than a month."

"Too early to tell what we were having," she said softly.

In the days since learning about the loss of our child, I'd spent countless hours wondering what he or she would've been, what they would've looked like. Would they have had a mixture of both of our temperaments, because that would've definitely been a lethal combination! I knew she would go through the hours of asking these questions as she continued to grieve, but I didn't want her to hurt right now.

"Iree told me to tell you that you and her are shooting the fade," I informed her.

"The only win she would get is if she beat a bitch while she's down. Where is everybody anyway?"

"Home," I replied.

"I'm surprised my parents didn't set up a base of operations right in the hospital."

"Well that's not possible for two reasons. One, they don't know you were shot, and I know you may be mad at me for keeping that from them, but I had good reasons," I said.

"I'm sure you did, but you can tell them I'm awake now, because I wanna see them and the kids."

"That's not gonna happen, and that brings me to reason number two. You're not in a hospital," I said slowly.

Hearing this made her beautiful eyes snap open and quickly take in her surroundings. She gave the room a once-over before looking at me, and then she looked around the room again before swinging her eyes back to me.

"Baby, are we where I think we are?" she asked slowly.

"Key West."

"Yeah, that's what I thought. Now, my memory is a little hazy, so I'm gonna need you to help me out a little bit. Isn't Florida the last place we want to be right now?" she asked.

"It's the last place anyone would expect us to be," I replied.

"I can tell I'm gonna need the full explanation, so go ahead."

"I'll give you the highlights. It turns out that it might not have been your baby's daddy who put the hit on you. I know the Columbians are involved, but that's probably only because of what I did to Pablo. I still don't know who the other person is, I just know that the person who took over for Pablo knows and I'm gonna ask him about it when I see him. Since I plan on that being much sooner than later, I decided that it was best to hide in plain sight, and I wasn't about to let you leave my side, so I had an in-home hospital built. That's not Patrón in your IV, that's morphine," I said.

"Whatever it is, it's heavenly. So, do they think I'm dead?"

"I don't know, but I don't think they knew it was you driving my car. Remember, that was the same car I was driving when I came to town for the original job, and it kinda sticks out if you're looking for it. I think they were trying to hit me for not getting the job done on you," I replied.

"They're some bold muthafuckas to come after you."

"I plan to explain that to them when I see them," I said, smiling.

"Okay, so what did you tell my family?"

"I told them we decided to extend our honeymoon, and they agreed to stay at the house. I told Iree what was really going on though, so she could keep her eyes open, since you did give her a gun," I replied.

"It seemed like a good idea at the time," she said, defensively.

"It was, baby."

"Aight, so if Joakeen wasn't behind it, then who the fuck was?" she asked, frustrated.

"I've been impatiently waiting on you to wake up so I could ask you that question."

"Well I don't know anybody else that's locked up out here, if that's still the angle you're working," she replied.

"That's all I have to go on, but now that you're awake, I can do some more thorough investigating."

"That sounds like you're about to leave me here while you run the streets," she said, clearly unhappy with that prospect.

"You won't be alone. The house is staffed with a cook and a maid, plus you have a nurse and doctor staying down on the first floor, so that you get constant monitoring and attention. Not to mention, the goons I've got guarding the perimeter."

"Won't they look out of place in this gated community?" she asked.

"The thing about living in a gated community is that you can do what you wanna do, because it means you've got the money it takes to be here. Besides, the neighbors think the owner of this house is a rapper," I replied.

"And who is the owner of this house?"

I gave her a smile that made her shake her head.

"This view alone had to cost you two million dollars," she said, looking out of the floor to ceiling picture windows at the clear blue water off in the distance.

"Closer to three million, but it's just money."

"Spoken like a muthafucka who has forgotten what it's like to be hungry," she said.

"Baby, I could never forget what it's like to have my ribs touching my back, which is why I have as much money put away as I do."

"And how much is that exactly?" she asked, smiling.

I smiled too, but I wasn't as concerned with answering her question as I was kissing her. I knew that she was still too fragile physically for any type of sexual intercourse, but I knew how to make love with my mouth.

"It's good to see our patient is awake," the nurse said, peeking her head into the bedroom.

I'd have to discuss the importance of knocking to her later on.

"Come in, Denise," I said, kissing Honey one more time before sliding out of the bed.

"I-I think I remember you," Honey said, looking closely at the short blonde approaching her.

"She was one of the nurses that saved your life," I clarified.

"Oh, okay, so you work at the hospital," Honey said.

"Well, I did," Denise replied.

"Don't tell me they fired you for saving too many lives," Honey said sarcastically.

"Nope, I quit. I mean, I kinda had to," Denise replied, smiling at me.

"Why?" Honey asked curiously.

"Because when a man shows up with half a million dollars in untraceable currency, you do what he says, and you do it with a smile," Denise said, laughing.

"That sounds like a move my husband would pull."

"Only the best for you, baby. Plus Denise managed to keep the cops away from you long enough for me to sneak you out of there," I said.

"Denise, don't let him corrupt you," Honey replied, smiling.

"Never would, but I do think it's amazing that he would do anything for you, and I respect that. So, I'm now your nurse until you no longer need me. What do you say we take a look at you?"

"Sounds like a plan," Honey replied.

"I'm gonna make a call," I said, kissing her one more time, before stepping outside on the upper deck.

I was more than grateful she was awake, but now it was time to get back to business.

"It's me," I said, when the phone was answered.

"What's the situation?"

"She's awake and the nurse is checking her now. What's the situation on your end?" I asked.

"It appears the info that cop gave you about ole boy's habits is accurate. He's flashy, arrogant, and believes he can't be touched."

"Oh, I could usually touch him from a distance, but I need answers. What are his weaknesses?" I asked.

"Like most men, it appears to be the women in his life. That would be his mother, grandmother, and daughter. Outside of them, the only thing he focuses on is working hard and playing harder. He is as crazy as they say though."

I wasn't worried in the slightest about the reputation a muthafucka had earned, because I knew I could turn that rep into a legacy they left behind. One of the universal truths in the world was that there was always a muthafucka who was bigger, badder, and meaner than the next man. For Juan Pedro, I was the huckleberry.

"Tell me about the women," I said.

"The mother and grandmother are pretty much homebodies, except when they go to church. The daughter is something like a Miami socialite. She's twenty-two, so she's heavy into the club scene."

I processed this information rapidly, knowing what had to be done.

"Put surveillance on all three and snatch them at the first available opportunity, after I let you know that I have him," I ordered.

"What's your play to get to him?" Aubrey asked.

"Make me an appointment this afternoon with his favorite escort, and pick a nice hotel for us."

"Sounds romantic," Aubrey said sarcastically.

"Trust me, when she hears my proposition, she's definitely gonna climax."

"Anything else you need done?" she asked.

"No, I'll call you with further instructions," I replied, hanging up.

I knew all too well it wasn't easy to bring a madman to his knees, but it was possible because whether he was insane or not, he loved who and what he loved. Juan Pedro was about to learn the hard way why it was safest not to love at all.

"Baby, is there a reason why both of those women are beautiful and from what I've been told, so are the cook and the maid?" Honey asked, smirking.

"I hadn't noticed, sweetheart, but you did say you like women," I replied.

"Uh-huh, just like I did say that I don't share, so if you were thinking about a threesome, you can forget it," she said.

"A threesome? What kind of man do you take me for? I absolutely was not thinking about a threesome. Now, if we're talking about an orgy, that's a whole different conversation," I replied, laughing.

The shock on Savannah's face made the situation funnier, and I could see my wife struggling through the pain as she chuckled.

"You're not funny, bae," Honey said.

"Really? Because I think I'm funny as fuck," I replied, moving back to her bedside.

"Well, try to keep your jokes to a minimum, so your wife doesn't open up her staples laughing," Savannah, her doctor advised.

"Speaking of which, I've heard that chopper bullets burn, but damn I didn't know they would cause a bitch to get staples!" Honey said angrily.

"I'm just glad you're alive," I said honestly.

"Don't worry, we're gonna keep her that way. Even if we have to give her a little mouth-to-mouth," Denise said suggestively.

"Oh, Lord," Savannah said, shaking her head as she followed Denise from the room.

Once they were gone, we just stood there looking at each other, saying so much without saying anything at all.

"Thank you for saving my life," she said.

"It's nothing you wouldn't and haven't done for me."

"True. I knew the paralyzing panic you felt though, and I know you don't do good with fear," she stated.

"No, I don't."

"Did you get the people who shot me?" she asked.

"The ones who pulled the trigger, yes."

"Tell me how you did it," she demanded.

"I managed to shoot and kill two of them in the middle of the melee, and I tracked the third one down after I got you to the hospital. I strung him up and used a whip to beat the flesh off his body, until it fell away like tender meat on a bone. Then, I poured gas on him and stood there while he burned to death."

"Sounds biblical," she replied, smiling.

"It was a good start," I admitted.

"Now what?"

"Now, I go get the answers that we need," I replied.

"Can you stay with me for a while? I wanna go to sleep feeling you next to me."

Without hesitation, I climbed back in the bed with her to fulfill her request. I held her until long after her breathing deepened from sleep, only getting up when I felt my phone vibrating. The text from Aubrey said I had an appointment with an attractive half-Vietnamese, half-Cuban woman named Jenny Woo in two hours, room 1090 of the Regency Hotel. There was a slight risk to moving around Miami since that was where Juan Pedro was the strongest, but I had a distinct advantage over him. He didn't know what I looked like. I took a quick shower before putting on a cream-colored Tom Ford suit and some matching Black Billionaire loafers. Once I had my Ruger .44 tucked, I grabbed an empty Louis Vuitton gym bag and made my way outside to my black 2020 Ferrari Spyder. I looked like money, I smelled like money, and a quick stop at the bank only enhanced those factors. I made it to room 1090 fifteen minutes late, but the look in Jenny Woo's eyes gave the impression that she was still more than willing to please.

"I'm sorry I'm late, I had to make a quick stop," I said, gesturing towards the bag in my hand.

"It's quite alright, your appointment is scheduled through until eight am tomorrow morning."

She stepped aside and allowed me to enter the room, and I could feel her observing everything about me.

"You come highly recommended, so I'm sure your time is very valuable," I said, taking a seat on the couch.

"It can be, but I promise I'm worth it."

"Oh, I have no doubts. I actually think you're worth more than what you charge by the hour, and that's why I've come to make you a proposition. A lucrative preposition," I said.

"Sounds interesting," she replied, taking a seat next to me.

"Trust me, it is. Tell me what you think about this," I said, passing her my Louis Vuitton bag.

Sitting it on her lap, she unzipped it and moved the contents around before looking at me.

"How much?"

"Two million," I replied.

"For that type of money, you must want me to kill somebody important."

"No, you're just gonna fuck him. I'm gonna kill him."

# Chapter 16
## Two days later

I could hear their faint laughter when they came through the front door, and the boisterous sounds of a man who had too much alcohol. Their conversation was moving in the direction of my hiding spot, but I wasn't worried because I knew I was the last thing on a nigga's mind at a time like this.

"I missed you," Jenny Woo said seductively.

"I bet you did, because nobody can fuck you like me," Juan Pedro replied arrogantly.

"I know, that's why I hate it when you make me wait so long."

The pout on Jenny's face had Juan Pedro hypnotized, making me shake my head at how painfully easy this shit was. I watched on in silence from my hiding spot in the closet of Jenny's penthouse bedroom, waiting patiently for my moment. Based on the conversation I'd had with Jenny, I knew I couldn't move with the same speed as I had when lying in wait for Tori Hynel, I had to let her go through with her seduction. Juan Pedro had two of his lieutenants with him and they always waited in the living room until the fucking began. Only when the unmistakable sounds of Jenny Woo's passion reached their ears, did they quietly exit and wait in the hallway. From what Jenny said, it was never a long wait either. That meant my window of action was about as small as Juan Pedro was. How a five foot five, two-hundred-pound, middle-aged, balding Columbian thought he could contend with a giant like me was mind-blowing, but he was damn sure gonna get what he'd been looking for. Jenny's striptease revealed a body equal in beauty to her face, and her performance was fitting for this last show. She'd been hesitant to betray a man so powerful and ruthless, but no woman wanted to sell their body if they didn't have to. Plus, I'd promised her that Juan Pedro would be too dead to retaliate or give any order of the kind. Being that I'd showed up with two million in cash, my word spoke for itself, and the fact that I hadn't insisted on getting what I paid for in terms of our appointment, spoke to my character. I really was Captain Save-A-Hoe. Despite the show Jenny had put on, she still had to get on her knees and use her mouth to get him hard. Seeing this had me suppressing the laughter that was bubbling in my throat, but it was okay because I knew there would be plenty to laugh about later. It took ten minutes of diligent work before Jenny achieved enough success to climb on top of Juan Pedro and begin riding him. Her performance was worthy of an Oscar, because I knew there was no way the passionate sounds that floated from her sexy lips, were actually being caused by what was inside of her. After a few minutes, I heard the front door open and close, and then Jenny's eyes discreetly found mine in the moonlight.

"I want you on top of me," Jenny declared passionately.

With a lot of grunting and labored breathing, they managed to change positions, but I waited until he was back inside her before easing the closet door open. I only stuck the barrel of the gun out, but I wasted no time pulling the trigger and popping him in his right ass cheek.

"Fuck!" he exclaimed, putting a hand on the wounded area.

I could tell the tranquilizer I hit him with was already taking effect though, because Jenny was fighting not to let his body hit the floor.

"Help me!" she whispered fiercely.

I quickly stepped out of the closet and helped her maneuver his body onto the bed.

"God, I'm so glad that's over," she said.

"I can imagine. You were good though."

"If you wanna know what good is, then put your dick in me," she said, spreading her legs in my direction.

Even by the moonlight I could see how pink her pussy was, but my thoughts were centered completely on the business at hand.

"Something tells me that if I do that, then we'll be in more than a compromising position. Don't forget we still got two muthafuckas in the hallway to deal with," I said.

"I know, I know. I'll go get them now."

When she left the room, I stepped back into the closet and waited. A few seconds later, two men rushed in the room, and went straight to Juan Pedro's side. I hit them with two shots apiece, dropping them instantly.

"Now, do we have time to fuck?" she asked, smiling once I was back out of the closet.

I laughed while shaking my head at her.

"You're too much for me."

"I have a feeling we would be evenly matched on this particular battlefield, and the more you say no, the more I want to find out," she said seriously.

"I'm flattered, but you need to put Florida in your rearview as soon as humanly possible, because shit is about to get ugly."

"I don't, I don't know how to thank you," she said, stepping towards me and giving me a hug.

"Trust me, it was my pleasure."

"No, but it could've been. Are you open to a compromise?" she asked seductively.

"What are you proposing?" she stared boldly into my eyes, while her finger worked my zipper and with the expertise of a pickpocket, she had my dick in the warmth of her palm. Much to her delight, I was hard within seconds and she quickly got on her knees. To say that she started to suck my dick is an understatement, because from the word go, she was gobbling me up. Her brown eyes blazed up at me with insatiable hunger as she caught a fast rhythm that had me playing ping-pong inside her throat. I'd never had my knees start knocking so fast, but it was obvious Jenny Woo was on a mission to taste victory. I wrapped my fingers up in her short black hair, moving my hips with the same determination as I would've, had I been in between her legs. I lost track of the minutes, but I knew it took me no time to erupt in Jenny's mouth, and she sucked me down like I was her favorite milkshake.

"J-Jesus," I whispered, fighting to maintain my balance.

Once she'd gotten everything out of me, she stood up and smiled at me.

"My pussy is ten times better than that," she bragged.

"Then I really can't fuck you, because I'd never let you leave."

"I don't know why, but even though I just met you, I'm tempted to stay," she confessed.

"That's not a good idea."

"On that we agree, but it would still be fun," she said, smiling wickedly.

I shook my head as I tucked my dick back into my pants, and got back to work.

"I need you to get Juan Pedro dressed while I take care of the other two," I instructed, grabbing my bag out of her closet.

Once I exchanged the tranquilizer gun for my real pistol, I tucked it into my pants and then dragged the two unconscious henchmen into her bathroom. I put them in the shower side by side, and gave them two bullets apiece to the brain. When I came back out of the bathroom, both she and Juan Pedro were dressed, which meant it was time to evacuate the building. The first thing that I did was make a call so the two dudes in the shower would be taken care of, and then I called to make sure my ride was downstairs. With all that done, there was really only one thing left to do.

"You got the suitcase?" I asked.

She left the room and returned a few moments later with the biggest Samsonite suitcase on wheels I'd ever seen.

"Oh, he'll definitely fit in there."

I swiftly shoved the little fat man in the case, zipped it up, and grabbed my bag.

"You ready?" I asked.

"As I'll ever be."

She led the way out into the living room where her luggage was, and then we made our way downstairs to the waiting Chevy Suburban idling at the curb. To any observer, we appeared to be a couple taking a trip, maybe even some people from out of town who were headed home, but definitely not accomplices of kidnapping, and murder. We loaded up quickly and vanished into the night. Everything had gone according to plan, which meant I only had one call left to make.

"It's me, everything is a go."

"I'm on it," Aubrey replied, hanging up.

"Is it strange to wish I'd met you sooner?" Jenny asked, looking at me.

"Only if it's strange for me to wish the same thing."

"I guess it's just funny how life works sometimes, because maybe if we had met sooner, I wouldn't be as fortunate as I am now," she said thoughtfully.

"Or maybe you would be more fortunate," I replied, smiling.

"How far away is your destination?"

"About twenty minutes, why?" I asked.

"Because I'm not wearing any panties," she whispered, smiling naughtily.

"We're not exactly alone."

"And?" she countered, dismissing the fact that the driver was no more than a few feet from us.

"I don't have a condom."

Like magic, a gold wrapper appeared in her hand, shining as brightly as her smile.

"This was your plan all along, huh? The compromise before was simply part of the seduction," I accused.

"If you want me to apologize, I'll tell you now that I can't do that. I've spent too much of my life having sex with men for every reason except the right one, but I want to be with you for the right reasons. I do not want to lay claim to you because I'm sure you belong to another woman, but I'd like to claim this moment as my own."

Maybe it was the fact that she was undeniably beautiful in that exotic way most men dream of possessing, or maybe it was the understanding that Honey was gonna be physically incapable of giving me what I needed right now. Whatever excuse I would use didn't matter, because I still held my hand out for her to give me the condom.

"Allow me," she said, swiftly moving onto my lap.

Within two deep breaths she had my dick out, the condom on, and she was easing us together until we fit in perfect harmony. I immediately understood two things. I understood why Juan Pedro had continued coming back, and I understood that as tight as she was, he hadn't been doing nothing inside her. I thought she was going to try and kiss me, but instead, she buried her face in my neck as she rode me slowly. I'd heard her performing earlier for Juan Pedro, but the authentic sounds of her passion were so much better. The way she moaned softly, almost like she was in pain, spoke to her not concentrating on a job and instead letting her body take over. It took a few moments for her pussy to fully open itself to me but once it did, the tempo increased, along with the heat building between us.

"I'm-cumming," she sighed softly in my ear.

Even with the condom on I could feel the splash every time she took me deep into her ocean. I could feel her teardrops on my neck too, but she moved with the same determination so I continued to hold her close, and enjoyed the ride. When she came again five minutes later, I couldn't hold back any longer, and dual sounds of fulfillment echoed through the SUV as my dick throbbed steadily inside her. Neither of us spoke a word and she didn't move for the rest of the journey to the safe house. When we pulled up out front the driver stepped out, giving us a few moments of privacy.

"Are you okay?" I asked.

"I think so, but there's really only one way to find out."

"What do you mean?" I asked, confused.

She started moving again to make her meaning clear.

"J-Jenny, you have to go," I said.

"Then make me c-cum," she whispered in my ear.

As I laid her down on the seat, I hoped that Magnum condoms were as reliable as advertised. I dove back inside her, putting her legs on the roof while showing her just what I was about. I rocked her hard for ten minutes, making her cum three times before the train ran out of track and I tumbled down the cliff behind her.

"How a-about now?" I asked, breathing heavily.

"Now I-I don't ever want to s-stop," she confessed, smiling.

I laughed and pulled out of her, happy to see that the condom was intact. Full, but intact.

"You've got a plane to catch, and I've got a man to kill."

"If you ever get out to the West Coast, look me up," she said.

"It's a date," I replied, opening the door and climbing out of the truck.

Tossing the condom, I went to the back and got my luggage before walking around to speak with the driver.

"Make sure she goes on the plane safely," I instructed.

The man nodded his head, got back behind the wheel, and pulled off.

"You could've brought her in the house, you know," a voice said out of the darkness.

I didn't have to see her to know this was the same petite black girl who was here last time.

"What's your name?" I asked.

"Rose."

"Well, Rose, I didn't think it would be appropriate to bring my personal situations into my business situations," I said.

"I was just letting you know because it's hard to really put your dick game down in a truck, but from the sounds of it, you handled your business."

"Glad you approve," I replied, laughing.

"No problem. So, what do you need first this time?"

"Let's hang my luggage out back, I'll deal with him in the morning," I said.

Suddenly, a flashlight came on at my feet and she turned to lead the way around back. Once I had Juan Pedro secured and guaranteed to hang around for a while, I followed Rose in the house.

"I got you a new whip because you got your money's worth out of the last one, and the machete you wanted," she said, pointing to the stuff on the kitchen table.

"What about the barrel of acid?"

"Yeah, it's outside and I already tested it," she replied.

For a second I just looked at her. Her face was plain, her hair was short, and her eyes were brown, which made her just like millions of other little black girls around the world. That statement had me looking at her different though.

"You tested it?" I asked.

"What? I know people that need killing too."

I put my hands straight in the air to signify I was leaving that alone.

"Can you order something to eat while I take a shower?" I asked, pulling money out of my pocket.

"No, I'll go pick something up. Anything in particular you want?"

"Surprise me," I replied.

"I've done that twice already tonight," she said, laughing softly.

I had no response for that, so I went in search of some hot water. Fifteen minutes later, I was feeling refreshed, and after my call to Aubrey updated me on the fact that my care packages would be arriving within the hour, I was feeling eager. In anticipation of being busy, I decided to call Honey while I had time.

"What are you doing, woman?" I asked.

"Sleeping, man, like most normal people do at this time of night."

"Oh, so now you wanna front like you're normal?" I asked, chuckling.

"Fuck you, Dollar."

I could hear the laughter through the sleep in her voice, and it gave me a warm feeling inside.

"I miss you," I said truthfully.

"I miss you too. Will I be seeing you soon?"

"I don't know, *maybe*," I replied.

"Maybe my ass, I'm tired of being cooped up with all these women," she said.

"Really? So you mean to tell me that Denise ain't eat your pussy yet?"

For a moment she was silent, and then I could hear her laughing softly.

"Dollar, that's not the point, the point is that I miss my husband, and I want you to eat my pussy," she stated.

"And I want you to suck my dick."

"You say that like somebody else has been doing it in my absence. I'm not gonna ask because I don't wanna know, and if you wanna keep your dick, you better make sure I don't ever know. Understand?" she asked aggressively.

"I understand, but do you understand that you're so sexy right now?"

"Glad to hear it. Now, go handle your business, and then bring your ass home so you can cum down my throat. I love you," she said.

"I love you too," I replied, laughing as I hung up.

"I hope you like Cuban food," Rose said, coming through the door.

"I'm good with that."

"How long before the rest of the crew gets here?" she asked, unpacking the food.

"Sometime within the hour is what I was told."

“So, what are you gonna do with them until morning?” she asked.

“I’ll think of something,” I replied, smiling.

# Chapter 17

"Rise and shine!" I said, swinging the whip in my hand with all my strength.

The sounds of the hard leather peeling the flesh off of Juan Pedro's back was music to my ears, and it gave me a reason to smile this early in the morning. I had no idea what he was yelling, but it sounded like Portuguese.

"Juan, I don't speak that shit, but I do speak pain!" I said, slicing through the thick meat of his back like a knife through warm butter.

"Do you all know what he's saying?" I asked, peeking around him to look at the three naked women that were nailed to the table a few feet away.

Saying they were nailed wasn't an accurate description though, because in actuality, I'd taken steel spikes and hammered them through both shoulders on each woman. The two older women had immediately passed out from the pain, but the young girl had remained lucid. This time I didn't have to ask for a translation, because there were chunks of shit falling from in between his ass cheeks faster than I'd ever seen any cow accomplish.

"Juan, you smell like beans!" I said, opening up another river of blood in his back.

"What do you want?" he finally asked, crying openly.

His question made me move around to where I could look him in the eyes.

"I want two things from you, Juan Pedro. The first thing I want to know is, who ordered the contract on Tabitha Dewhit?"

"Who?" he replied.

I slowly walked over to the table and stood directly behind Juan Pedro's grandmother.

"Juan, I don't know if Grandma can take this, but we're about to find out," I said.

The sound of the whip cracking against her back was like a rock being thrown through a piece of paper. I could tell by the way her body slumped that she'd passed out quicker than a little black lady in a Baptist church, but I popped her again, just because of the look on Juan's face.

"Daddy, please!" his daughter begged, crying hysterically.

"What's it gonna be, Juan?" I asked, moving one step over so that I was behind his mother.

"I don't know!" Juan yelled.

"You're lying, Juan," I sang out.

I did a quick wind-up and then I opened up his mother's back like a dropped watermelon.

"Juan," his mother called out weakly.

"I gotta be honest with you Juan, the two older women ain't built for what I'm gonna put them through, but your daughter is young and she can take it. Can't you, sweetheart?" I said, caressing her firm ass cheek gently.

Through the pain on Juan Pedro's face came a murderous rage I'd seen in many men before.

"If I didn't know any better, Juan Pedro, I'd think you didn't like the way I was touching your little girl," I said, deliberately running my finger in between her pussy lips while he watched.

"Get the fuck away from her!" he yelled, struggling to get free.

I slowly stuck my finger in my mouth while looking him dead in the eyes.

"She tastes so good though," I said calmly.

"Daddy, do something, *please*!" she begged, crying harder.

For a second, I thought that I was getting through to him, but there was still too much defiance in his eyes for my liking.

"Tell you what, Juan, you think it over while I take a break," I said, letting the whip drop to the ground.

He tried to hide his relief, but he was a bad actor. I slowly unzipped my jeans and pulled my dick out, stroking it and never taking my eyes off of Juan Pedro. When I was hard, I moved back down to where his grandmother lay unconscious, stepping right up behind her.

"Wait—"

That's the only word that got to pass his lips before I was balls deep in her pussy. She was dry, but tight, and her sudden grunts made me believe she remembered how this dance went.

"Stop! Stop! Okay! I talk!" Juan Pedro screamed.

"Wait until I'm done with my break," I said, holding onto her hips while moving faster.

For a full two minutes, I watched the destruction build in his eyes, and then I stopped.

"You started out dry, but the water still works don't it, old girl?" I said, smacking her on the ass.

One step to my left moved me down the line.

"I will tell you what you wanna know, just please stop!" Juan Pedro begged.

When I pushed my dick inside his mother's pussy, the tears he'd been fighting finally fell to his cheeks, but that still didn't stop me.

"D-damn, you're w-wet," I said, pleasantly surprised.

Within five minutes, her pussy did the unthinkable by suddenly spasming into a climax that had her moaning through her tears.

"Yo, Juan, your mom just came on this dick," I said, laughing as I pulled out of her.

Another step to my left brought me to the supple flesh of the tasty young lady that had inspired this brilliant idea of mine.

"Daddy!" she screamed, her voice shaking with terror.

"It was Anthony Benelli! Anthony Benelli ordered the contract, I swear!" he screamed insistently.

"You wouldn't lie to me, would you?" I asked, slowly invading his daughter's tight, hot slippery pussy.

"Oh, God! Dad, he's in me! He's in me!" she screamed in a full-blown panic.

"I'm not lying! I'm *not lying*!" Juan Pedro yelled instantly.

I stopped moving long enough to pull my phone out, and call Aubrey.

"Run the name, Anthony Benelli," I said when she answered.

"Can you hold on for a second?"

"I can try, but I'm in some *really* wet, *really* tight pussy right now, and I've been trying not to cum since the last bitch came on me," I replied honestly.

"I'm afraid to ask," she said, laughing.

"Trust me, you don't want to know."

"I probably don't, because it sounds like someone over there is crying," she replied.

"Well, if they're not crying, then I'm not having any fun," I said, punctuating my sentence with a pounding stroke of my dick.

"D-Daddy!" she wailed.

"Oh wow, you really are doing the most right now. Aight, Anthony Benelli was doing time, courtesy of the state of Florida, but it looks like…yeah, he was paroled a couple weeks ago," Aubrey said.

"Any connection to my wife?"

"Not that I can see, and it's gonna take me some time to track his movements," Aubrey replied.

"Aight, well get on it, and call me when you got something," I said.

"I got you. Have fun."

"I will," I replied, laughing.

I hung up and put my phone back in my pocket.

"Y-you got what you want, now get away from them," Juan Pedro demanded.

"I told you that I wanted two things from you, Juan."

"What else? What else do you want?" he screamed.

I waited until he was starting directly into my eyes before I answered.

"I want to break you," I said.

With my intentions made clear, I began to savagely fuck his daughter, making sure I smiled in his face the entire time. She screamed until she lost her voice, but in the end, her body succumbed to the inevitable chemical reaction caused by sexual intercourse. Unlike with her grandmother though, I didn't stop fucking her when she came, instead, I used her own natural lubrication to wedge my dick inside her tight little asshole. I could tell immediately this was her first time and with every blow, she grunted like her great-grandmother had. Her asshole made quick work of me, forcing me to cum within minutes, but that was okay because once Juan figured out I wouldn't stop, he'd closed his eyes to it. After wiping my bloody dick on her ass, I put it away and picked the whip back up.

"Time to get back to work," I said, pausing for a moment to admire my handiwork.

The look in Juan's eyes was complete and utter defeat, but that still wasn't enough to make me quit. I put the whip down on the table next to the dead woman, and picked up the machete from in front of her. I stepped in front of his mother and raised it high with the intention of burying it in her brain, but Rose stopped me.

"Haven't you realized you won?" she asked, from her seat on the steps by the back door.

"You must always crush your enemies completely."

"Look at him, and tell me you haven't accomplished that," she replied.

I didn't have to turn around to know what look was on Juan Pedro's face, or what was in his soul.

"Why do you care?" I asked.

"Because killing needs to serve a purpose, Dollar. What purpose is served by continuing to torture any of them, when you've already got the information you need and there's somebody else who obviously still needs killing?"

"Because I like torturing people," I replied honestly.

"I respect your candor, but you're obviously doing all of this for an important reason. This ain't business for you, it's completely personal, and that's fine. That just means you can't lose sight of your goal, because if you do, it could cost you more than you wanna pay."

The truth in her words was undeniable, and I had to admit that, no matter how badly I wanted to continue on my present course of action.

"So, what are you suggesting?" I asked.

"Kill them all, and move on to the next."

"Grab the acid," I said, putting the machete down, and grabbing the sledgehammer.

Starting with Juan's mother, I beat the spikes through her shoulders until she collapsed to the ground, and by that time

Rose had wheeled the fifty-five gallon oil drum full of acid over to us.

"Just let them go," Juan Pedro said.

"This is the life you chose for them, so you have no right to ask that they be spared," I replied.

To avoid getting acid splashed on me, I pulled out my gun and put a bullet in both women's brains.

"I can get them in there, why don't you finish him off?" Rose suggested.

Picking the whip back up, I made my way over to Juan Pedro.

"You had to know it would come to this, Juan, I mean, you undoubtedly heard stories about me. But, even if the stories didn't deter you from making your move, you still broke the number-one rule of engagement. You took your shot and missed," I said.

"One day it will be you that hangs from a tree as you watch your loved ones tortured and defiled. Karma will get you."

"Probably, but you won't be here to witness it," I replied smiling.

I beat him with the same intensity that I had his hitta and his grandmother, and when he passed out, I woke him up by cutting his dick off. Finally, after an hour, he earned the ballet that laid him to rest. I unhooked him from his restraints, and added him into the stew that was his family tree.

"Has anybody ever told you that you're deep?" I asked Rose.

"I'm gonna assume you're talking about my intellect and not my pussy, so I thank you for the compliment."

Her response had me shaking my head while cleaning up all traces of what had happened here today.

"Damn, it's noon already," I said, shocked, looking at my phone.

"Yeah, you were off in your own world, and I was determined to leave you alone for the most part."

"I kinda get caught up sometimes," I replied truthfully.

"It's cool. Are you gonna take a shower?" she asked.

"Nah, I'll do it when I get home."

"No offense, but you stink and I know your dick is dirty. I don't think you wanna go home to your wife like that," she said seriously.

"Point taken, I'm going to hop in the shower."

I made my way back inside the house, but before I got in the rain box, I sent Honey a text that I would be home soon. With that done, I took a leisurely thirty-minute shower, feeling sore, but good overall and ready to finally finish this shit up. I wanted Honey to live in peace and never have to look over her shoulder, but I had no illusions about me ever being able to afford that luxury. Death was coming for me like it was everybody else, but my clock was accelerated and my time was stolen, instead of being borrowed. I laughed at Honey's response telling me to bring her lips and her dick home immediately, and that I better not even stop to get something to eat. I sent a big blue thumb emoji, got dressed, and went to find Rose.

"Everything straight?" I asked, coming into the living room.

"Everything is good with me, how 'bout you?"

"I got one more piece of business to handle and then I'll be good," I replied.

"Stay focused."

"I will and I'll stay in touch too. I like you, Rose. We'll definitely work together again."

"I'm always down for that," she replied, smiling.

I grabbed my bag, went out to my car, and got in the wind. I didn't realize how hungry I was until I started seeing different fast food chains, but I'd told my baby I was coming straight home and so that's what I did. An hour and a half later, I was easing the car into my driveway, nodding at the two niggas posted up in the black Tahoe in front of my house. As soon as I walked through the door, I smelled something cooking that made my stomach growl and shake with excitement and expectation, but the food quickly became a secondary thought as I caught sight of my wife sitting at the kitchen counter.

"Well, look who's up and moving around," I said.

The smile on her face and the way her eyes lit up melted my heart instantly, and I immediately stepped into her open arms.

"Hi, baby," she said happily.

"Hi, beautiful," I replied.

"Thank God you're home," Denise said.

"Yes, because this one right here cannot deal with you being gone," Savannah said, pointing at Honey.

"Talk about separation anxiety," Denise continued.

"Will you two bitches shut up," Honey said, laughing.

"Oh, there is no way he doesn't know you're whipped by now," Savannah said, laughing.

"Whipped, huh?" I asked, smirking, looking down at her.

"Fuck you, Dollar," she said, elbowing me.

"Awww, baby, it's okay to be whipped because in all fairness, the dick is amazing," I replied.

"I would call bullshit on that, but I gotta say I believe you. I mean, I know I can eat some pussy, but I only kept her attention long enough for her to squirt in my face, and then we were back to talking about you," Denise confessed.

Hearing this had me laughing hysterically, which of course earned me another elbow.

"Once again, you bitches can shut up anytime now," Honey said laughing too.

"Relax, girl, we're not gonna talk about the threesome," Savannah said softly.

"Wow!" I exclaimed, giving my wife a look of shock.

"Don't look at me like that, I almost died. I needed to feel alive again," Honey said defensively.

"Shit, if that excuse works, then I'm good, because I got shot before you did. So, which one of you wants to fuck?" I asked, looking back and forth between the two women. Both of their hands shot up immediately, which made us three laugh, and made Honey elbow me harder.

"Bae, please don't make me cut a bitch," Honey said.

"I would never. I'm just glad that you're obviously healing and feeling better," I said sincerely.

"I can't lie, you chose good people to take care of me, and I'm not just saying that because of their tongue skills either," she replied.

"That's good to know," Savannah said sarcastically.

"So, what is smelling so good, and who's cooking?" I asked.

"That would be braised beef with white rice, steamed broccoli with cheese sauce, rolls, apple pie for dessert, and your wife is doing the cooking," Denise replied.

"Damn, baby, you doing it like that?" I asked.

"Only for you, my king," she replied, pulling me towards her until our lips met.

"And that's our cue," Savannah said.

I was too busy wiping my mouth to show Honey how much I truly missed her to pay attention as to whether or not they left the room. Just being in the presence of this woman was like coming in out of a storm, and I never got tired of the way she made me feel.

"Wait 'til after we eat," she said, stopping my hand's journey into her shorts.

"Then you better feed me quick."

I reluctantly took a step back so she could get up and go to the stove. Seeing her limping took me from loving to homicidal mad before I could draw a deep breath.

"So, are we done in Florida? Can we go home now?" she asked.

"Almost, I just gotta see one last man."

"Who?" she asked.

"Anthony Benelli."

The sound of the pan she'd been holding as it hit the floor had me moving towards her in a hurry.

"Bae, what is it?" I asked.

"Anthony-Anthony Benelli is who you're looking for?"

"Yeah, do you know him?" I asked.

"He's my-my-my father."

# Chapter 18

If I hadn't been right on top of her to catch her when she passed out, she would've ended up holding the floor like they had an ongoing love affair. Part of my brain was still trying to process the last words she'd spoken, but they weren't computing. I'd thought I heard her say Anthony Benelli was her father, but I was gonna need her to repeat and explain, before I was convinced I wasn't tripping.

"Denise! Savannah!" I hollered, scooping my wife up into my arms.

"What happened?" Denise asked, running into the kitchen.

"She passed out. Turn the stove off and both of you meet me upstairs," I demanded, already heading in that direction.

My chest was so tight I thought I might be having a heart attack, but somehow I knew it was just that blind panic, wanting to take over. Honey being hurt in any kind of way always inspired this reaction in me, and no matter how much I hated it, I knew I was helpless to change it. I loved her. I carried her quickly upstairs and laid her in her bed, looking at her face closely for any signs of distress.

"Baby," I said, gently stroking her cheek.

"Is she breathing?" Savannah asked, hurrying into the room.

"Yeah, she's breathing," I replied.

"What happened?" Savannah asked, moving to the other side of the bed checking her vitals.

"We were talking. I said something that shocked her and then her lights went out."

"Try this," Denise said, coming into the room with some smelling salts.

I moved out of the way so she could get to Honey and within a few moments, she had her eyes flickering open.

"What the fuck-fuck is that smell?" Honey asked, shaking her head vigorously.

Denise, Savannah, and I let out collective sighs of relief. I could tell that Honey was disoriented, but once her eyes locked on mine, I saw clarity hit her like a lightning bolt.

"What the hell did you say that made her faint?" Savannah asked curiously.

"You two do a complete check-up on her to make sure that that's what really happened and be thorough," I instructed, pulling my phone from my pocket.

I stepped outside on the upper deck and quickly called Aubrey.

"Talk to me, sis."

"I've got good news and bad news. The good news is that Anthony Benelli is still in Florida, and it shouldn't be hard to pin down his exact location. The bad news is that the word is already out that Juan Pedro and his family are missing," she replied.

"Well, we knew it wouldn't take long for that to happen."

"Yeah, but we also figured that by the time that happened you'd be putting Florida in your very expensive rearview mirror. Something tells me that's not exactly your plan now," she said.

"You're right it's not. Have you found any connection between dude and my wife?" I asked.

"None and I've looked in all directions I can think of. What did your wife say?"

"Some shit that doesn't make sense. When I said his name, she said that was her father and then she passed out, but I know that can't be right because I met her father before, two weeks ago," I said.

"Hold on for a minute."

I had no idea what Aubrey was doing, but I could hear her fingers flying over a keyboard with the speed of a machine gun. While I waited, I observed Savannah and Denise standing on either side of Honey, asking her questions. I could tell she was answering them, but her eyes were fixed on me and her expression was unreadable. It hadn't been too many occasions when I didn't know what was going on in that beautiful mind, but now was one of them.

"Dollar, how old is your wife?" Aubrey asked.

"Thirty-eight, she'll be thirty-nine at the end of the year. Why?"

"Because, almost forty years ago, Anthony Benelli went to prison. For rape," she said slowly.

"Tell me you're not saying what I think you're saying," I replied.

"All I'm doing is speculating, but it would explain her reaction."

"Yeah, but it wouldn't explain his actions, I mean if that's his daughter, why the fuck would he try to kill her?" I asked, struggling to find the logic.

"I don't know, but I'd say it's a safe bet that your wife does."

When I looked back through the window and my eyes locked with Honey's, the blank look she'd been giving me suddenly vanished, but all that was left was pain. So much pain.

"I think you're right, Aubrey."

"So, what's our next move?" she asked.

"I want you to find Anthony Benelli, because I intend to drink his blood from a wine glass with my dinner."

"What about the Columbians?" she reminded me.

"Get word to them that Anthony betrayed Juan Pedro, and that I'm gonna handle that situation for them, free of charge," I replied, smiling.

"Nice. I'll call you when I know something."

I hung up just as Denise and Savannah were leaving the bedroom, so when I stepped back inside, Honey and I were alone. Before saying anything, I went and closed the bedroom door to ensure that we had privacy, and then I crawled in the bed next to her. Despite wanting answers, I knew this wasn't my conversation to start, and so I patiently waited for her to say something.

"I'm cold. Will you hold ne?" she asked softly.

"Of course, baby."

She turned on her side, putting her back to me, and I pulled the blanket up around us while wrapping myself around her.

"I'm sorry I didn't finish cooking, but I will though," she said.

"Shhh, it's not important. All I want and need is you."

"Do you really mean that?" she asked, unsure.

"With all my heart."

"But what if-what if I—"

"The what ifs don't matter, sweetheart, so let's not entertain them," I said.

I could feel her body trembling against mine, and I knew it wasn't from the cold now as much as it was the chill of whatever memory she was trapped inside. In a lot of ways, I was a textbook sociopath and I was okay with that, because feeling cold could only make me more effective at my job. My love for this woman made me feel what she felt though.

Knowing in part what she was trying to work up to tell me had me wondering how she would feel about me if she'd known how I spent my morning.

"H-how much do you know?" she asked softly.

"Only enough to draw the conclusion he still needs to die."

"He deserves to die," she said passionately.

"I'm working on it, bae, trust me."

"I do trust you, and that's why I'm gonna tell you an ugly truth. My ugly truth. The man that you know as my dad is my dad in every sense of the word, but I was conceived by another man's sperm, and that man didn't give my mother a choice. It was rape. I'm ashamed and I never wanted you to know, so that's why I never said anything," she said.

"That shame isn't yours to carry, sweetheart, because you don't do anything wrong. Your birth has been a blessing to so many people that you should never be ashamed, and you better not ever think I'm gonna love you any less or look at you differently. To me, you'll always be the definition of what Tupac meant when he said a rose grows from concrete," I replied, holding her tighter.

For a while neither of us said anything, but the silence wasn't uncomfortable or awkward. There was too much love in the air.

"You're my everything," she whispered.

"And you're mine."

"I didn't think I'd ever find my soulmate, I mean I believed you were out there, but I've been through so much that I—"

"I'm here and I'm all yours. I promise," I said, kissing her softly on the neck.

"Thank you, Dollar. I mean that."

"No, thank you, baby," I replied sincerely.

I understood there was sadness and pain inside her that I might not be able to fully get rid of, but I was damn sure gonna do my best to try. I was just about to ask her why her piece-of-shit sperm donor wanted to kill her, when I felt her getting more comfortable beneath the blanket. I didn't say anything when I felt her reach back in between us and unzip my pants. It went without saying that she could do what she wanted, and that's exactly what she did. Within seconds, she had me hard enough to hold up the Golden Gate Bridge, and she slipped me inside her with a sigh of long awaited satisfaction coming from both of us. My right hand found its way in between her legs to her clit, and the combination of rubbing it while plunging my dick deep in her was like steadily turning the faucet on a sink. I had to let her set the speed and rhythm we danced to, because the last thing I wanted to do was hurt her. With every stroke, it became clearer that I could fuck all the women in the world, but my Honey was still the best.

"P-put a b-baby in me," she stammered, moving faster.

"I will."

"Y-you promise?" she asked emotionally.

"Yes, baby," I said, pounding her just a little harder.

When she came a few minutes later, I stopped moving suddenly.

"Why-why did you stop?" she asked.

"Shhh, just wait."

I could feel her frustration just as surely as I could feel her pussy thumping with the same intensity as her heart, but I knew her body so I waited. When the aftershocks had subsided a little, I dove inside her fast and hard, giving her long pleasurable strokes that had her clutching my arm in a death grip.

"O-oh-okay, daddy!" she moaned in surrender.

I tried not to overexert her, but it was still a long, thirty minutes of good loving before her pussy released its hold on me.

"D-don't make me go that long without that," she said seriously.

"I won't, especially not if I'm gonna keep my promise."

She slowly unfolded from my embrace so she could turn around and lay facing me.

"You sure you wanna have a baby with me?" she asked, searching my face intently.

"Absolutely positive."

"Are you gonna rub my feet when they're swollen?" she asked.

"Bae, I married you, so that means I signed up to wipe your ass when you can't. What's a foot rub compared to that?"

"That's the most disgusting, yet romantic thing I've ever heard," she replied, laughing.

I kissed her thoroughly to let her know I was serious, regardless of whether it was disgusting or not.

"I need you to promise me something else," she said.

"What is it, baby?"

"I need you to promise to keep me safe during my pregnancy. I know you can't control everything that goes on in the world, and I know you have to work, but I need you to make sure the baby and I are safe," she replied.

"You already know you don't have to ask me that twice, but I need your help though."

"How?" she asked.

"I need to take care of Anthony, which means I need to know everything I can about him. For starters, why does he hate you enough to send a muthafucka like me after you?" I asked.

"That requires a little back story. So, when you asked me about knowing anyone else who was locked up, I told you no because as far as I knew, Anthony was still on the run. A few years ago, he'd gotten busted for trying to sell kids on the black market, and for some insane reason, he thought it was my fault he got busted. Maybe because a few days before that, I'd gone to his house to rescue my sister from the hell he was putting her through and—"

"Wait, what sister is this?" I asked.

"Oh yeah, I have a half-sister named Amanda, a few years younger than me."

"You're just full of surprises," I said.

"Stay focused, bae. Aight, so Anthony got hemmed up or whatever, but he made bond and disappeared, and I ain't heard shit about him since. For obvious reasons, I try not to think about him."

"Well, I know you didn't tell on him, for one that's not who you are, and for two Aubrey would've found that during her digging. He should know that same thing though because he's obviously connected, so there has to be another reason that he's coming at you," I said.

"Does it matter?"

"Absolutely not because I'm gonna kill him regardless, I'm just trying to figure out his thought process so I can better project his movements," I replied.

"What do you mean predict his movements? I thought that he was in prison."

"No, he got out a couple weeks ago," I admitted.

"Where-where is he?" she asked hesitantly.

"All I know right now is that he's somewhere in Florida, but I don't have an exact location."

I could see her doing some heavy thinking, but once again I had no idea what it was about. It didn't make sense that she was worried about him getting to her here, but fear was never a rationale thing.

"What's your plan?" she asked.

"If everything is going according to plan, then Anthony has lost the support of the Columbians, which means his protection has diminished greatly, and that should make it easier to kill him."

"When are you going after him?" she asked.

"Once I get you back to Mississippi."

"Dollar, I—"

"If you're about to give any justification, rationalization, or explanation as to why I shouldn't take you back to Mississippi, you don't even need to waste your breath," I said seriously.

The pout she gave me was sexy, but it wasn't enough to move me. Not on this issue. As if on cue, my phone started ringing, forcing me to pull it from my pocket and answer.

"Yeah?"

"I know where he is," Aubrey said.

"Hold on," I replied, getting out of the bed and taking the call outside.

I knew Honey had those renegade tendencies, so I couldn't put it past her not to do some ill-advised shit if she knew where to find this muthafucka.

"Aight, tell me what you got," I said.

"He's in Fort Lauderdale. Apparently, he hooked up with a rich white bitch while he was inside, and now he's living the lifestyle of the rich and famous."

"Where is he now?" I asked.

"At home in her twelve-million-dollar mansion, but I know he made a dinner reservation for two for nine pm tonight."

I looked at my phone, not liking that I only had about six hours to get Honey to safety, and be back here. That meant I was gonna have to improvise.

"Aight, listen, I'm gonna put my wife in a car that needs to take her straight to my house in Mississippi. No stops, no detours, nothing! When you arrange it, I want you to explain to the driver that I don't give a fuck if my wife puts a gun to their head, they better not stop the goddamn car," I stated adamantly.

"Understood. What else do you need?"

"I want you to get in touch with the owner of the restaurant and buy it out for tonight, whatever it costs. The only people who eat in that restaurant are Anthony and his date, and if they have surveillance cameras, I want you to make sure they're taken care of. If it's a closed circuit system, then I'll deal with it when I get there," I said.

"It's awful short notice to shut an entire restaurant down," Aubrey replied skeptically.

"Make them an offer they can't refuse, and text me the restaurant location," I said, hanging up.

I understood the risks to doing business this way, but sometimes guerilla tactics were the only tools left in the box. I could see the questions in every beautiful smile line on Honey's face when I came back in, but past experience had taught me to tell her what she needed to know.

"I need you to get dressed," I said.

"Why?"

I just looked at her because I knew she knew the answer to that question.

"Come on, bae, get dressed," I said again.

"We don't keep secrets from each other, Dollar."

"Is this really an argument you think you can win using that logic?" I asked, smirking.

The flash of anger in her eyes was instant, yet beautiful. It also didn't move me.

"You know why I've kept certain shit from you," she said, irritated.

"Likewise."

"But this—"

"Anything after but is bullshit, so please don't kick it my way. Now get dressed," I said, forcefully.

Her laying there and crossing her arms in defiance made me put my phone in my pocket, pull my pistol from the small of my back, and eject the clip.

"Baby, you know I love you, right?" I asked, putting the clip in my pocket.

"Yes, Dollar, I know that."

"And you know I would do anything for you, right?" I asked sweetly, swiftly ejecting the bullet that was in the chamber.

"I'm not scared of you."

"Nor should you be, but you should be mindful of the fact that my love for you knows no bounds. No bounds. So you can either willingly get dressed or so help me God, I'ma put a part in your head with this pistol as I smack you to sleep," I vowed, moving towards her.

She actually had the balls to stare me down for a moment, but seeing she couldn't win this battle forced her to angrily toss the blanket aside and get out of bed. When she bent over in front of me, giving me a wonderful view of her ass and pussy in order to put her shorts back on, I knew she was only a little mad. I wouldn't be enticed by sex, not even mind blowing, face numbing sex.

"Are you happy now?" she asked sarcastically.

"You've made me happier than I can ever remembering being," I replied truthfully.

I knew she wanted to be mad with me, but her heart was in her eyes and it erased all doubts of anything except unconditional love.

"I-I'm scared of what will happen if I'm not by your side," she said emotionally.

"I get that, and I love you just as much, but we both know what can happen when I'm distracted. I took my eye off the ball once in this situation already, and you almost died because of it. I need you to understand that I can't do that again."

"I understand…and I'll leave. Just please come home, because I don't know who to be any more if I'm not Mrs. Malcolm Joyner. You're my-my whole world," she said, crying steadily.

I tucked my gun and pulled her possessively into my arms, holding her as tightly as I could without hurting her. No words would do, so I just held her until she was all cried out.

"There's a car coming to get you, but I'm starving, so can we go back downstairs and finish our meal?" I asked.

"I'd like that," she replied, smiling up at me through the remaining tears in her eyes.

With her hand in mine, I led her back to the kitchen where we were pleasantly surprised to find instructions directing us to our finished meal that was warming in the oven. After forcing Honey to take a seat, I fixed our plates and joined her at the table. Our conversation wasn't about death and killing, but instead it was about what was next for us. There was no doubt in either of our minds that our life together would be the definition of an adventure, and we were in agreement about that being the best type of life to live. The fact that I could love a woman who knew me and didn't want to change me in the slightest, gave me a feeling of peace that was indescribable. Before Honey, I hadn't believed in the notion that there was someone for everyone, but now I knew that was as true as my aim. Towards the end of our meal, I got the text that her ride was here, and I could see sadness wanting to overtake her again. I refused to let that happen though, and before Honey knew what was happening, she was in an intense make-out session with Denise and Savannah.

"So, you bitches are just gonna send me away with a wet pussy and without my man?" Honey asked, smiling despite her frustration.

"Blame your husband, it was his idea," Denise said.

I put my hands up like they were full of shit because I had nothing to do with it.

"You do know I'm still gonna need medical attention, and there is plenty of room at the other house, so…" Honey said, smiling in a way that I was all too familiar with.

Suddenly, I was under intense scrutiny of all three women.

"I don't know what you all looking at me for, if you wanna go you better get your shit, because the car is waiting," I said.

The two women immediately disappeared, leaving me alone with my favorite girl.

"Why are you so good to me?" she asked, putting her arms around me.

"Because you deserve it. Just try not to get caught by your parents or the kids."

She couldn't help laughing at that.

"I'll do my best, and since you're so good to me, I might let you have all of us one time when you get home," she said seductively, kissing my lips in a way that promised many things.

Before I could respond, Denise and Savannah were back, snatching her from my arms and pushing her towards the door.

"I love you, baby!" Honey said, giggling.

"We love you, baby!" they mimicked in unison.

"I love you too!"

I watched as they got in the car and pulled off, then I sent Aubrey a text, letting her know it was time to get everything else underway. I went upstairs to change my clothes and to load my new Glock .40 with the one hundred drums, known as monkey nuts. I had no idea what I was walking into, but I'd be prepared for whatever. When I finished loading the first gun, I quickly loaded my silenced Ruger .350, and made my way to the car. I had Aubrey on traffic cam surveillance to make sure Honey stayed on track, and so I could drive as fast as I wanted to. I pushed my Ferrari to the limit and before long I was pulling into the back of the Herringbone Restaurant. My drive-by to get a look at the front revealed only a few cars, which meant Aubrey had made the impossible happen. Now, it was my turn.

# Chapter 19

"Good evening, Mr. and Mrs. Benelli, how is the food this evening?" I asked, stopping at their table.

"I'm not Mrs. Benelli," the young blonde replied, annoyed.

"But, why not? You certainly look better than her," I said.

"Exactly!" she exclaimed.

"Hey, pal, we're good here so you can move along," Anthony said.

"Do you feel like he's ashamed of you, or he wants to have his cake and eat it too?" I asked the girl, while completely ignoring Anthony.

"Honestly, I don't know what it is, but I'm getting sick of it," she replied.

"Shut up, will you? And you, get lost," he demanded, pointing a finger at me.

"What's your name, beautiful?" I asked.

"Holly," she said, smiling at me.

"What the fuck are you telling him your name for? He's the help, for Christ's sake! And you, if you don't get your black ass back in the kitchen, you won't be working here much longer. I'm a preferred customer, that's why they shut the restaurant down just for me, so you better do what I say," he threatened angrily.

"Actually, it was me who had the restaurant shut down for you and the beautiful Holly," I stated calmly.

"You did? Why would you do that?" Holly asked with curious fascination.

"He's lying, babe, only people with real money have that kind of juice," Anthony said, smirking.

“Oh, I’ve got money and when it comes to juice, you can just call me Sunny D. Allow me to introduce myself, my name is Dollar,” I said, taking Holly’s hand and kissing the back of it.

My eyes never left Anthony’s face, and it was clear by the sudden bulge of his eyes that he knew exactly who I was.

“Dollar, as in money?” Holly asked.

“The very same. I’m about that almighty dollar, unless something else catches my interest,” I replied, letting my eyes skate over her in a way that made her blush.

When I turned my glare fully on Anthony, I noticed the sweat on his upper lip and the sudden twitch in his right eye. There were certain facial features I could tell he’d passed along to Honey, and that only further enraged me, but I maintained my outward calm.

“You okay, Anthony?” I asked, smiling.

My question made Holly look at him too, and even put a hand to his forehead like a mother would a sick child.

“You’re hot,” Holly said, frowning.

“No, sweetheart, you’re hot,” I said, looking at her.

That frown instantly vanished and out came a girlish giggle that fit in with her early-twenties age range.

“C-can we get back to our dinner p-please?” Anthony asked politely.

“Almost everyone is entitled to a last meal. Almost,” I replied, no longer smiling.

“I feel like you two know each other or something,” Holly said, looking back and forth between me, and the sack of shit sitting next to her.

“You wanna tell her how we know each other, Tony?” I asked.

“I don’t-I don’t know you,” he replied shakily.

"Sure you do, or at least you know of me. I'm the muthafucka you sent to kill your daughter," I said, taking a seat across from them.

"Wait, you have a daughter, and you tried to kill her?" Holly asked in disbelief.

"I-I don't know what he's talking about," he said.

"So, you're calling me a liar?" I asked softly.

The look on his face telegraphed the understanding that there was no good way for him to answer that question, but by now he should've realized it didn't matter what he said. His ass was grass.

"Anthony, is he telling the truth?" Holly asked.

"Yeah, Tony, am I telling the truth?" I asked.

"I-I don't-I didn't mean to. It was Juan Pedro—"

"Let me stop your stuttering ass right there, Anthony, because Juan Pedro and I had a long talk before he died, so I know you're full of shit. You were the one pushing the issue to get your daughter killed, and when it didn't happen fast enough, you somehow convinced Juan to come after me. I can promise you that him, his daughter, his mother, and his grandmother are right now cursing your existence. Of course, they're doing it in the afterlife," I said, smiling widely.

"Y-you killed Juan Pedro?" he asked, now wearing a look of terror."

"His daughter, mother, and grandmother too," I replied softly.

Holly's sudden gasp reminded me that she was still with us.

"Holly, do you love Anthony?" I asked.

"No, I just use him for his money."

"Anthony, pull out all the money you have and your car keys," I instructed.

When he simply stared at me, I calmly reached inside my suit jacket and pulled out the .380.

"Make me repeat myself, I dare you," I growled through clenched teeth.

Suddenly, his billfold and car keys materialized in Holly's hands.

"Holly I want you to listen to me. I would appreciate if you got up and left this restaurant and forget that you ever saw me, or knew Anthony Benelli. Can you do that?" I asked, never taking my eyes or gun off of him.

"I can, I can do that," she replied.

"Holly, I'm not someone you ever want to see again because if you see me again, the clock that is your life will have just expired. Do you understand?" I asked slowly.

"Yes," she said quickly.

"Have a good night, Holly," I said.

She didn't so much as glance in Anthony's direction, sliding out of the booth and hauling ass.

"Alone at last," I said, sighing contentedly.

"Wh-what do you want? Money? How much?"

"You see that's your problem right there, you're stupid. If this was business, then I would've executed Tabitha hours after accepting the job, but you've been too blind to see that this is personal to me. That she is personal to me. Maybe if you would've stopped to think it through, you wouldn't be in this situation," I said.

"She's a junkie whore, how personal can it be?"

"Personal enough that you'll know agonizing pain before you die," I vowed.

"Look, we can work something out, I—"

Before he had a chance to move or finish his sentence, I smacked him out of the booth with the pistol. Predictably, he tried to run, but I double-tapped two bullets into the back of each knee which made crawling his only resort. I didn't mind watching him crawl, especially since he was headed towards the kitchen. I knew he probably expected to find some employees there who would help him, but the moment their food was done cooking, I'd cleared everybody out and shut all the cameras off before wiping them clean. No one had ever been here on this night.

"Help! I need help!" he yelled, in a frightened panic.

"There's no one home, Tony, it's just us and the secrets that these walls will never tell."

My honesty didn't stop him from slithering across the floor, any more than it silenced his pleas for help, but neither thing bothered me.

"Let me help you out," I said, grabbing him by his shirt collar and dragging him into the cooler.

"You see, Tony, the good thing about you picking this particular restaurant is that they actually butcher their own meat on-site."

When I tossed him to the floor, he looked up at all the beef and pork hanging on hooks, and the blood quickly drained from his face.

"Please-please, I'll give you anything—"

"Bitch, you better not think to beg me for your miserable fucking life," I growled, kicking him in the mouth savagely.

While he concentrated on not swallowing his tooth, I tucked my gun away, and pulled the zip ties from my pocket. I quickly secured his hands and feet to limit his resistance, then I took a slow look around to contemplate my next move.

"You know, on the drive out here, I thought about doing all types of shit to you but to be honest, none of it seems like enough because in the end, you'll still only die once. I don't like to simply kill a man, I like to break him, you know? The problem with a muthafucka like you is that you're less than nothing, so there's no one who loves you now, and no one to miss you when you're gone. Your life and death will be an insignificant footnote in somebody's history. How do you feel about that?" I asked.

"F-fuck you! Tabitha won't forget me and neither will her mother!"

"You know what? You just gave me a brilliant idea of how to kill you. Wait right here," I said, laughing as I went in search of the tools I would need.

It wouldn't equate to the hours of torture that I got to put Juan Pedro through, but it was poetic and sometimes that was worth more. Once I found what I was looking for, I put Tony up on top of one of the huge metal tables and pulled his pants down.

"Tony, I'm not gonna lie to you, you're about to get fucked, but the good news is that you're probably used to it with your bitch ass," I said, laughing joyfully.

"Wait—"

I didn't wait for him to beg, I waited for him to scream as I shoved the butcher knife in his asshole. He didn't disappoint, but his screams were high-pitched and a little off-key. Still beautiful though. I treated his asshole like it was my favorite piece of pussy on its period, and I pounded that knife into it long after my entire arm was covered in blood and shit. When he stopped screaming, I checked to see if he was still breathing and I was relieved that I hadn't killed him yet, because I didn't want him to miss the best part. Dropping the knife, I quickly flipped him over so he was lying on his back, and then I picked up the meat cleaver.

"I hope this thing is as sharp as it looks, but if it's not that's okay. Just be cool and don't lose your head," I advised.

His eyes barely flickered open, but I knew he saw what was coming as I raised the cleaver high over my head and brought it down on his Adams apple. Blood splattered like I dropped a bottle of ketchup from twenty stories up, but I didn't mind. The blade was sharp, but it still took me a half an hour of diligent chopping to get his head to roll away from his body. It was about three to four more hours before I had the rest of his body broken down enough to fit in the industrial strength garbage disposal, but it was fun work. Once that was done, I spent the necessary hour and a half cleaning up any traces we'd been there, before wrapping Anthony's head up, tossing it into my Louie bag, changing my clothes and leaving.

It had originally been my plan to go back to my house in Key West, but I decided to drive through the night to get home to the woman I loved. It was 11 am before I pulled up in my driveway, and I could barely keep my eyes open, but there was nowhere I would've rather had been.

"When the hell did you get a Ferrari?" Iree asked, once I'd made it from the car to the front porch.

"There you go, all in my business."

When she stood up, I saw the black Berretta 9mm in her hand, but I didn't flinch.

I dropped my bag at my feet and opened my arms wide.

"It's good to see you, Dad," she said, stepping towards me and giving me a hug.

"I missed you, Daughter. I heard you've been up to no-good too."

"Me? Up to no-good? I have no idea what you're talking about," she said, chuckling.

I kissed her on the forehead before taking the gun from her and tucking it into the waist of my shorts.

"I appreciate you holding shit down while I was gone."

"I only did what you expected of me," she replied.

"I still appreciate it. Why don't you and Rain get out for a little while?" I said, handing her my keys.

"Are you serious?"

"Don't wreck my shit, Iree, or I'll be forced to shoot you again," I warned.

She gave me a quick kiss on the cheek before running in the house screaming for Rain. I picked up my bag and followed her inside, going straight for the bedroom I knew Honey would be in. Despite all the noise Iree was making, my beautiful wife was sleeping peacefully. I knew the smile on her face either meant she was dreaming of me, or Denise and Savannah had thoroughly fucked her. My odds were on the latter.

"I see you're a man of your word, Dollar. Thank you," Mrs. Dewhit said, hugging me tightly.

I hugged her back and when I looked down the hall, I could see her husband sitting at the dining room table. He nodded his head in appreciation and I returned the gesture.

"Is she safe now?" Mrs. Dewhit asked.

"Yes, and I'll die to keep it that way," I replied truthfully.

"We don't wanna lose you either, so you two keep each other safe," she said.

"Yes, ma'am."

She squeezed me tightly one more time before letting go and going back to her husband. When I turned my focus back towards the bedroom, I found the most beautiful eyes I'd ever seen staring back at me, with a gorgeous smile to match.

"You were faking sleep, weren't you?" I asked.

"No, I was sleep, but the sound of your voice woke me up. I just prayed I wasn't dreaming and that you were really here."

"I'm here, baby, in the flesh if you wanna touch me," I said, grinning.

"Shhh, you know my parents are out there," she whispered smiling.

I could've pointed out that this was my house, but instead I held out my hand towards her.

"Take a walk with me."

She quickly got out of the bed and laced our fingers together, allowing me to lead her out the front door. We were just in time to see Iree turn the car around, get it straightened out in the driveway, and gun the engine until they shot off down the road.

"You actually let her drive your Ferrari?" Honey asked in disbelief.

"It's just a car. I did tell her that I'd shoot her if she wrecked it though."

"Yeah, well she already learned the hard way how serious you are when it comes to that," she replied, laughing.

"Facts."

"So, where are we going and why are you still carrying your travel bag?" she asked.

"Stop asking so many questions, and just walk with me."

She made sure to smack me on my ass, but she still followed my lead. I kept our stroll at a leisurely pace because it felt good just to be able to take our time for once. Life had been non-stop chaos, but now we could hopefully establish some normalcy in our life.

"So, I was thinking. How do you feel about us taking a vacation before I get back to work?" I asked.

“Baby, you already know that I’ll go anywhere with you. I do think we should wait until I’m completely healed though, especially if we’re going out of the country.”

“Is that your way of saying you wanna spend more time with the doctor and the nurse?” I asked, chuckling.

“Oh, whatever! You already know I prefer your company to theirs.”

“Sure you do,” I said sarcastically, causing her to smack me on my ass again.

“We did have a conversation about them relocating,” she informed me.

“Oh yeah, to where?”

“Wherever we need them. Savannah is a surgeon, but she’s studied medicine in general her whole life. Denise is the same way. If we let them stay at the house here, maybe volunteer at the local hospital, but always be on call should we ever need them, I think it’ll make sense in the long run,” she replied.

“Uh-huh, and does this mean you want to keep fucking them too?”

“Baby, you’re all I’ll ever need, but there’s nothing wrong with having a little fun,” she said, smiling mischievously.

“Do I get to have fun too?” I asked.

“To be honest, I want to be fair about it, but I don’t know if I can handle watching you fuck another woman. That’s gonna be a trial by fire, but I’m comfortable with finding out with these particular women.”

“Aight, well that’s something we can worry about later. For now, let’s focus on us,” I said, stopping and taking a seat right near the edge of the creek.

“I’m always focused on us, bae. I love you.”

"I love you too, and I brought you a gift as a token of my love," I replied, passing her the bag.

She took a seat next to me, put the bag in between her legs, and unzipped it. For a moment, she just stared at the head in the bag, and then she started laughing. When her laughter took on a hysterical pitch, I got a little worried, but she got herself under control.

"I didn't expect you to bring me a souvenir. Where's the rest of him?" she asked.

"Nobody knows."

"Someday you'll have to tell me what happened, but for now, I've got a better idea," she said, pulling the head out of the bag and sitting it on the ground.

"What, do you wanna play soccer?" I asked when she stood up.

"Maybe later."

When she started taking her clothes off, I knew what she had on her mind for right now.

"You're serious, huh?" I asked.

"Yep, we're gonna fuck and he's gonna watch. Now get naked."

"Whatever you say, baby, I'll do anything to make you happy."

# Chapter 20

## One week later

"It's me."

"I figured you'd be calling sooner or later, no matter how much shit you talk about needing a vacation," Aubrey replied, giggling.

"Oh, I'm still going on vacation, but my wife is still spending time with the family."

"Yeah, and you're about ready to come out of your damn skin from sitting still," she said, knowingly.

"Psychoanalyze me later, but put me to work now," I demanded.

"Aight, I'll call you back within the hour."

When I hung up, I felt some of the tension lift off my shoulder, and I was able to take a much-needed deep breath. It wasn't that I didn't like spending time with my wife and in-laws, but killing to me was like what smoking was to other people. A habit.

"Knock-knock," Iree said, from outside the door to my study.

"What's up, Daughter?"

"Nothing much, I just wanted to talk to you," she replied, coming in and taking a seat.

"That sounds serious."

"Ain't it always," she said, smiling ruefully.

"Aight, let's hear it," I said, picking up my blunt out of the ashtray and relighting it.

"So, I've been doing some thinking. Despite all the bullshit and drama, I love my mom with all my heart, but I don't think it's a good idea to live with her anymore."

“And where were you thinking about living?” I asked, releasing a cloud of smoke from my lungs.

“Here, with you and Honey.”

“You know Rain won’t be living here, right?” I asked, smirking.

“Relax, it was only sex. Good sex, but we’re not planning to get married. Besides, I want to be here to be around you more.”

“Me? You know I’m barely here,” I said.

“I know this is the most you’ve been here since you bought this place, and I know your wife loves it here. That means you’ll be down here more often than not.”

I wanted to argue with her, just because of the shit-eating grin on her face, but I knew her logic was sound.

“You know you’d have to go to school, right?” I asked.

“I’ve already sent in the paperwork to enroll in an all-girls’ school out here.”

“Oh, so you just knew I was gonna say yeah, huh?” I asked.

“No, she knew I was gonna say yeah,” Honey said, coming in the room and sitting in my lap.

“Ah, so the fix was in,” I said, shaking my head.

Iree laughed, but when I looked at Honey, I could tell she’d been crying.

“What’s wrong, baby?” I asked, concerned.

“Nothing, I’m good.”

I passed the blunt to Iree and nodded for her to leave us alone.

“Baby,” I said.

“Nothing’s wrong, I promise. I just found out my little sister is getting out of prison because her case was overturned.”

“You’ve got a sister in prison?” I asked, shocked.

"Amanda, the half-sister I was telling you about. She was inside for some dumb shit, but she gets out tomorrow."

"Well, that's great, baby," I said, smiling.

"The only problem is that she doesn't have anybody except me, so I kinda told her I'd be in Tennessee to pick her up in the morning," she replied hesitantly.

"Okay, so what's the problem?"

"I don't wanna take that drive by myself, and I was kinda hoping you'd go with me," she said.

"We all ain't fitting in that Ferrari, bae."

"So, we'll rent a car. Please?" she asked, giving me her sexiest pout.

"Now, you know damn well I can't tell you no," I replied, laughing as I shook my head.

"Thank you, baby! I'll take care of all the arrangements, you just keep handling business," she said, hopping up out of my lap, and running from the room.

I was still shaking my head as I sent Aubrey a text, telling her to hold on scheduling an appointment because my wife had tricked me into a road trip. Of course, her text back was a bunch of crying laughing emoji's, but I didn't feed into her bullshit. An hour later, Honey reappeared, took me by the hand, and led me out front to the waiting 2020 dark blue convertible Mustang.

"I packed us a bag already, and there are two guns in it. I'll drive," she said, going around to the driver's side.

"I'm just along for the ride," I replied, getting in.

Despite it being a spur-of-the-moment trip, I was still enjoying just being alone with my lady. We sang songs to each other, teased each other mercilessly with sex, and laughed until tears ran down our faces. By the time we got to Nashville, it was only a couple hours until her sister's release, so we didn't bother renting a motel room. Instead, we parked on a dead-end street and fucked like animals.

"If she asks why we're late, I'm blaming you," Honey said, pulling up in front of the prison.

"I'll gladly take my charge, because your pussy is worth at least five to ten."

"You struggle to last that long," she replied, laughing, hopping out of the car.

"You'll pay for that later!" I yelled after her.

She flashed me a devilish smile and blew me a kiss. I got out of the car to stretch my legs, and get rid of all the fast food wrappers. Since I knew it had been awhile since Honey saw her sister, I thought it would only be right that I sit in the back seat, and give them space to bond. For that, I needed not to be sitting on the remains of our McDonald's and KFC drive-thru massacre. I was so focused on cleaning and moving shit around that I didn't even notice them walk back to the car.

"Bae, this is my sister, Amanda. Amanda, this is the love of my life," Honey proclaimed.

I stood up, expecting to see a slightly different version of Honey, but I got a different type of surprise. I could see the resemblance to the man I'd killed a week ago. At the time I'd thought the familiarity I'd noticed in him was because of Honey, but I'd been wrong, so very wrong. Amanda's eyes were dark brown, almost black, but the confusion was easy to see. So was the anger.

"Why would you bring him?" Amanda asked.

"What do you mean? I told you my husband would come with me," Honey replied, confused.

"Your-your husband? Is that a sick joke?" Amanda asked angrily.

“And why did you call her Amanda?” I asked, looking at Honey.

“I called her Amanda because that’s her name and no, this ain’t no goddamn joke, this is my husband! Do you two know each other?” Honey asked, looking back and forth between us.

Neither of us spoke, probably because the truth was simply too weird to accept. I mean, I knew the world was small, but not this damn small!

“The last time I saw her, she was going by the name Katie,” I said.

“And the last time I saw him, he gave me this,” Amanda said, pointing to the scar from the bullet in her neck.

“He-he shot you? You-you shot my sister?” Honey asked in complete disbelief.

“Yeah. At the time I didn’t know she was your sister, though,” I replied, still staring at Amanda.

“Why would you shoot her at all?” Honey asked.

“Because I broke his heart,” Amanda said.

“Because you were my wife and you broke my heart…”

To Be Continued…
Soul of a Monster 2
Coming Soon

# Submission Guideline

Submit the first three chapters of your completed manuscript to ldpsubmissions@gmail.com, subject line: Your book's title. The manuscript must be in a .doc file and sent as an attachment. Document should be in Times New Roman, double spaced and in size 12 font. Also, provide your synopsis and full contact information. If sending multiple submissions, they must each be in a separate email.

Have a story but no way to send it electronically? You can still submit to LDP/Ca$h Presents. Send in the first three chapters, written or typed, of your completed manuscript to:

**LDP: Submissions Dept**
**Po Box 870494**
**Mesquite, Tx 75187**

*DO NOT send original manuscript. Must be a duplicate.*

Provide your synopsis and a cover letter containing your full contact information.

Thanks for considering LDP and Ca$h Presents.

**Coming Soon from Lock Down Publications/Ca$h Presents**

BOW DOWN TO MY GANGSTA

By **Ca$h**

TORN BETWEEN TWO

By **Coffee**

BLOOD STAINS OF A SHOTTA **III**

By **Jamaica**

STEADY MOBBIN **III**

By **Marcellus Allen**

BLOOD OF A BOSS **VI**

By **Askari**

LOYAL TO THE GAME **IV**

LIFE OF SIN **III**

By **T.J. & Jelissa**

A DOPEBOY'S PRAYER **II**

By **Eddie "Wolf" Lee**

IF LOVING YOU IS WRONG… **III**

LOVE ME EVEN WHEN IT HURTS **III**

By **Jelissa**

TRUE SAVAGE **VII**

By **Chris Green**

BLAST FOR ME **III**

DUFFLE BAG CARTEL **IV**

By **Ghost**

ADDICTIED TO THE DRAMA **III**

By **Jamila Mathis**

A HUSTLER'S DECEIT 3

KILL ZONE **II**

BAE BELONGS TO ME III

SOUL OF A MONSTER II

By **Aryanna**

THE COST OF LOYALTY **III**

By **Kweli**

SHE FELL IN LOVE WITH A REAL ONE **II**

By **Tamara Butler**

RENEGADE BOYS **III**

By **Meesha**

CORRUPTED BY A GANGSTA **IV**

By **Destiny Skai**

A GANGSTER'S SYN II

By **J-Blunt**

KING OF NEW YORK V

RISE TO POWER III

COKE KINGS II

By **T.J. Edwards**

GORILLAZ IN THE BAY III

**De'Kari**

THE STREETS ARE CALLING II

**Duquie Wilson**

KINGPIN KILLAZ IV

STREET KINGS 2

PAID IN BLOOD 2

**Hood Rich**

SINS OF A HUSTLA II

**ASAD**

TRIGGADALE II

**Elijah R. Freeman**

MARRIED TO A BOSS III

**By Destiny Skai & Chris Green**

KINGS OF THE GAME III

**Playa Ray**

SLAUGHTER GANG II

**By Willie Slaughter**

**Available Now**

RESTRAINING ORDER **I & II**

By **CA$H & Coffee**

LOVE KNOWS NO BOUNDARIES **I II & III**

By **Coffee**

RAISED AS A GOON I, II, III & IV

BRED BY THE SLUMS I, II, III

BLAST FOR ME I & II

ROTTEN TO THE CORE I III

A BRONX TALE I, II, III

DUFFEL BAG CARTEL I II III

By **Ghost**

LAY IT DOWN **I & II**

LAST OF A DYING BREED

BLOOD STAINS OF A SHOTTA I & II

By **Jamaica**

LOYAL TO THE GAME

LOYAL TO THE GAME II

LOYAL TO THE GAME III

LIFE OF SIN I, II

By **TJ & Jelissa**

BLOODY COMMAS I & II

SKI MASK CARTEL I II & III

KING OF NEW YORK I II,III IV

RISE TO POWER I II

COKE KINGS

By **T.J. Edwards**

IF LOVING HIM IS WRONG…I & II

LOVE ME EVEN WHEN IT HURTS I II

By **Jelissa**

WHEN THE STREETS CLAP BACK I & II III

By **Jibril Williams**

A DISTINGUISHED THUG STOLE MY HEART I II & III

LOVE SHOULDN'T HURT I II III IV

RENEGADE BOYS I & II

By **Meesha**

A GANGSTER'S CODE I &, II III

A GANGSTER'S SYN

**By J-Blunt**

PUSH IT TO THE LIMIT

By **Bre' Hayes**

BLOOD OF A BOSS **I, II, III, IV, V**

By **Askari**

THE STREETS BLEED MURDER **I, II & III**

THE HEART OF A GANGSTA I II& III

By **Jerry Jackson**

CUM FOR ME

CUM FOR ME 2

CUM FOR ME 3

CUM FOR ME 4

An **LDP Erotica Collaboration**

BRIDE OF A HUSTLA **I II & II**

THE FETTI GIRLS **I, II& III**

CORRUPTED BY A GANGSTA I, II & III

By **Destiny Skai**

WHEN A GOOD GIRL GOES BAD

By **Adrienne**

THE COST OF LOYALTY

**By Kweli**

A GANGSTER'S REVENGE **I II III & IV**

THE BOSS MAN'S DAUGHTERS

THE BOSS MAN'S DAUGHTERS II

THE BOSSMAN'S DAUGHTERS III

THE BOSSMAN'S DAUGHTERS IV

THE BOSS MAN'S DAUGHTERS **V**

A SAVAGE LOVE **I & II**

BAE BELONGS TO ME I II

A HUSTLER'S DECEIT I, II, III

WHAT BAD BITCHES DO I, II, III

SOUL OF A MONSTER

By **Aryanna**

A KINGPIN'S AMBITON

A KINGPIN'S AMBITION **II**

I MURDER FOR THE DOUGH

By **Ambitious**

TRUE SAVAGE

TRUE SAVAGE II

TRUE SAVAGE **III**

TRUE SAVAGE **IV**

TRUE SAVAGE **V**

TRUE SAVAGE **VI**

By **Chris Green**

A DOPEBOY'S PRAYER

By **Eddie "Wolf" Lee**

THE KING CARTEL **I, II & III**

By **Frank Gresham**

THESE NIGGAS AIN'T LOYAL **I, II & III**

By **Nikki Tee**

GANGSTA SHYT **I II &III**

By **CATO**

THE ULTIMATE BETRAYAL

By **Phoenix**

BOSS'N UP **I , II & III**

By **Royal Nicole**

I LOVE YOU TO DEATH

**By Destiny J**

I RIDE FOR MY HITTA

I STILL RIDE FOR MY HITTA

By **Misty Holt**

LOVE & CHASIN' PAPER

By **Qay Crockett**

TO DIE IN VAIN

SINS OF A HUSTLA

By **ASAD**

BROOKLYN HUSTLAZ

By **Boogsy Morina**

BROOKLYN ON LOCK I & II

By **Sonovia**

GANGSTA CITY

By **Teddy Duke**

A DRUG KING AND HIS DIAMOND I & II III

A DOPEMAN'S RICHES

HER MAN, MINE'S TOO I, II

CASH MONEY HO'S

**By Nicole Goosby**

TRAPHOUSE KING **I II & III**

KINGPIN KILLAZ I II III

STREET KINGS

PAID IN BLOOD

By **Hood Rich**

LIPSTICK KILLAH **I, II, III**

CRIME OF PASSION I & II

By **Mimi**

STEADY MOBBN' **I, II, III**

By **Marcellus Allen**

WHO SHOT YA **I, II, III**

**Renta**

GORILLAZ IN THE BAY **I II**

**DE'KARI**

TRIGGADALE

**Elijah R. Freeman**

GOD BLESS THE TRAPPERS I, II, III

THESE SCANDALOUS STREETS I, II, III

FEAR MY GANGSTA I, II, III

THESE STREETS DON'T LOVE NOBODY I, II

BURY ME A G I, II, III, IV, V

A GANGSTA'S EMPIRE I, II, III, IV

**Tranay Adams**

THE STREETS ARE CALLING

**Duquie Wilson**

MARRIED TO A BOSS… I II

**By Destiny Skai & Chris Green**

KINGS OF THE GAME I  II

**Playa Ray**

SLAUGHTER GANG II

**By Willie Slaughter**

**BOOKS BY LDP'S CEO, CA$H**

TRUST IN NO MAN

TRUST IN NO MAN 2

TRUST IN NO MAN 3

BONDED BY BLOOD

SHORTY GOT A THUG

THUGS CRY

THUGS CRY 2

THUGS CRY 3

TRUST NO BITCH

TRUST NO BITCH 2

TRUST NO BITCH 3

TIL MY CASKET DROPS

RESTRAINING ORDER

RESTRAINING ORDER 2

IN LOVE WITH A CONVICT

**Coming Soon**

BONDED BY BLOOD 2

BOW DOWN TO MY GANGSTA

Printed in the USA
CPSIA information can be obtained
at www.ICGtesting.com
LVHW021107141123
763810LV00044B/811

9 781951 081096